AWAY WITH A STRANGER

ALSO BY MELANIE GREENE

Dunway Siblings Series

Feather in Her Cap *(Jeannie & Brendan)*

Twelve Scorching Days *(Sarita & Scorch)*

Margo of the Bells *(Margo & Karl)*

Pier 3 Coffee Series

Mocha for Mateo *(Alicia & Mateo)*

Cappuccino for Callie *(Abraham & Callie)*

Latte for Leyla *(Austin & Leyla)*

Curiosity (Amity & Josh)

Polar Opposites *(Audra & Salt)*

Roll of the Dice Series

Rocket Man *(Serena & Dillon)*

Ready to Roll *(Janice & Miguel)*

Eye of the Tiger *(Natalie & Evan)*

Let the Good Times Roll *(Chloe & Gabriel)*

Roll of a Lifetime *(Rachel & Theo)*

Roll Play *(Kim-ly & Tómas)*

On a Roll *(Gillian & Vic)*

Roll in the Hay *(Anton & Cisco)*

AWAY WITH A STRANGER

MELANIE GREENE

To Mally, who shines

CHAPTER
ONE

COLE

I wasn't running late; I'd checked an app telling me how long it would take to get from the central concourse to my departure gate. The text about my flight boarding had only just chimed.

And my newborn nibling surely needed a onesie with Philly's iconic LOVE sign on it, no matter how long the gift shop's line was taking. Sure, I'd mailed back gifts from various local merchants for both of Larissa's kids, and for all of my sisters, but my heart screamed that this tiny little outfit was an essential add-on.

Should I get a matching shirt for Larisa's oldest? But the line was six-deep behind me, and the couple insistently pushing into my personal bubble didn't give the impression they'd let me dash over to grab a 2T and regain my spot.

So fine, Alfie Junior would have to be content with the sea-life book, the silk play scarf, and the Gritty puppet. But his sibling needed just one more gift before I returned to Rockport for my first Christmas since moving out of Texas.

Onesie secured, I powered through to the gate. The first group wasn't even boarding, what with the typical increase of families with small children traveling during the holiday season, so I wove my way to a spot by the windows overlooking our plane to Houston. I had a three-plus hour drive once the three-plus hour flight ended, so I wasn't in a hurry to get strapped into seat 26C.

I planted myself in the only spot clear of people shuffling to line up or tethered to the one bank of working outlets, bending to zip the gift into my carry-on. Which is when someone side-swiped my ass, testing the results of my gym time. Of course I passed, not being a man who skipped leg day, but that smug thought only took me so far as I turned to the interloper.

They were hunched into themselves and pacing, and it took me a sec to place them. "Andi?"

Andi Ennis swung to face me. Blinked those beguiling eyes of theirs, which were currently fogged with some kind of stress or unhappiness. "Um. Hello? Oh, Cole, hi."

"You okay?" Pointless question; all of their effortless panache was missing. Their outfit was almost boring in its simplicity, and instead of their usual topknot showing off their multihued undercut, their hair was frizzed out all around Andi's whiter-than-normal face. But their appearance wasn't what was disconcerting; it was the buzz of unhappy energy that kicked me into 'figure out how to help' mode.

Andi nodded, which I didn't believe for a second.

I gave their forearm a quick squeeze. "Okay, good. Are you flying to Houston, too?"

"Ha. Well. Not sure I have a choice now. I can't get past all these people to the customer desk to ask, and even if I could, what would I even do, and if I don't, what would that mean about the whole rest of my life?"

There were still people folding strollers around the

ticket-check counter, and a short line of others who seemed to be gate-checking their carryons. I backed to the window, giving them some space, and made what I hoped was a trustworthy face. "Maybe tell me the situation, and talking it out will make it clear?"

Andi sighed heavily, letting their backpack thud to the ground beside my roller bag. "This isn't—I'm not feeling there's much to make clear. I mean, I know what's happening. I don't know my next steps, is all."

"And what's happening?"

The look they shot me wasn't entirely suspicious. Just ... wary. And, okay, it's not like Andi knew me all that well, but we had half a dozen acquaintances and friends in common. We'd been at the same parties, and bars, and Jerome's over the top post-Thanksgiving brunch.

"Fine. Yeah. I'm supposed to be going to Houston. Well, Clear Lake, it's this suburb ..."

"I know Clear Lake." I'd been to college with people from there. Parts of it were probably fine, but others reminded me of all the 'cons' in my 'should I move away from my family / Texas' pro-con list.

"Right, you're from, what, Corpus?"

"Rockport, but, yeah." My little beach town was quickly merging with the city of Corpus Christi just to the south, but was still clinging to its independent identity.

"Okay, yeah. The plan was Christmas with my stepmom and half-sisters, and I'm here and dealt with all the airport hassle and two minutes before they call boarding, she tells me her new boyfriend's just moved in and—okay, sparing you the exact words, but basically, it's either I show up ready to perform a gender for them, or I don't show up at all."

TWO

ANDI

Of all people to get me to spill my woes all over the runway.

Not that I had anything against Cole Dunway. Jerome raved about him, and Jerome read people like it was his superpower. But it wasn't my habit to go around exposing my soft innards to anyone, especially someone I thought about in full-name terms.

Also, I'd heard of at least three incidents where he went into do-everything-my-way-it's-the-best mode while acting like he was some kind of laid back, chill and neutral party.

His next statement shouldn't have taken me aback. "You can come stay with me instead."

"What, in Rockport?"

"Well, unless you want to go to your stepmom's? I thought the point was you don't."

I snorted. "I do not. Not with those rules." Not when it seemed like whatever this new guy in her life brought to the table, it freed her up to unleash the crap opinions she used to mostly keep away from me.

"Of course not, it's too disrespectful, and probably they'd keep crossing lines. So, I don't know how long your trip's for, but I'll be staying with my family until the twenty-sixth, and you're more than welcome."

I narrowed my eyes at the customer service desk, which was almost accessible now they were boarding the first group of passengers. "I'm going to see about canceling my ticket."

Shouldering my backpack, I left him to his spot against the windows. He was still standing there, all solid and secure in his family's welcome and the promise of holiday cheer, when I returned.

"Did it work out?"

I shook my head. "If I try to leave now, with my bag checked and already on board, they'd have to unload everything and delay departure by however long, and then she went into a whole thing about the holidays and tight schedules and I gave up."

"What if I take charge of your bag in Houston? I could just hang on to it?"

"I asked that." He looked surprised at my, what, audacity? Like I would hesitate to volunteer him without advance notice, when desperation to get out of all this was sinking me under a layer of stress molecules? "It's no good. We're not on the same reservation, so they wouldn't trust I'm not being nefarious, even if you did trust me."

"Of course I trust you."

"Not the point, Cole. Thanks, I mean, but from the airline's perspective, you're no good to me."

He crossed his arms, then shucked his coat and re-crossed them. He was so damn comfortably embodied, and ready for phase two of his tell-me-how-to-go-on pitch. "Listen, my parents have a beach cottage down the lane from the house. It's my year to stay there—I don't know if you remember, but I've got five sisters. Most of them don't live in Rockport, so we use the cottage for overflow when everyone's in town. I'm happy to share, and I've been plenty comfortable on the sofa in the past. If you don't want to hang with my family, you can walk the beach, borrow a car and go wherever, stay in and binge some shows, no pressure."

"No pressure." I deadpanned, waiting to see if he'd blush about giving me the hard sell.

He didn't so much as duck his head sheepishly. "Exactly. And if you want to hang, we're a good bunch. I'll vouch for them respecting you."

Right, as if he was authorized to make that guarantee? As narrow minded and conservative as Clear Lake could be, at least it was part of one of the nation's largest and most diverse urban areas. Small town Texas, though? People like me got out of places like that for a reason.

Cole himself must have left for a reason. I knew he'd changed his ID, started hormones, and gotten top surgery while living in Texas, but that was no proof that his family wasn't part of the problem. Despite the casual claims he made about his literal handful of sisters.

Why would I believe he wasn't glossing over a mess of gender essentialism, since he'd taken the trouble to get his own ass out of town?

He sighed at me. Like, actively, pointedly, at me. "Come on, Andi. What else is your plan? Get to IAH, turn around, and fly right back here?"

If I weren't an affable person, I'd have growled at him. Because yes, that was another idea I'd had to reject. My roommate's cousin was already moved into my room for the holiday. Everything I thought of, besides Cole's solution, would cost me so much cash and—I could admit to myself, but no one else—would leave my sneaky brain way too much alone time.

I did not need my sneaky brain to come up with stories about all the reasons I was alone at Christmas.

"Does this beach hut have Wi-Fi?"

THREE

COLE

As soon as we landed and took our phones off airplane mode, I sent Andi the notes I'd made. Neither of us had had seat mates willing to trade so I could fill them in about my family, and I didn't want them overwhelmed with all our names and traditions and plans once we got there. So I spent the flight typing up a notated family tree, and flipping between various text threads and calendar appointments to compile a timeline. Decorating cookies, the tamalada, Aunt Maxima's toy drive, prepping for the Dunway Christmas party, the party itself.

All that was only if Andi wanted to join in. I'd seen how skeptical they were about their welcome, but my people would prove themselves soon enough.

A whole string of texts popped up. Thirty-two just from Jerome. It seemed he'd heard about my invitation from Andi and wanted to fill my screen with all kinds of opinions. Their stepmother embodied Grimm archetypes. They had a thing about being friendly instead of speaking their mind. They'd probably never mention how they don't like mushrooms. Not allergic to it or anything, just not their favorite thing.

Cole: Babe, I got this. I won't stress them out.

Jerome: You will, though

Jerome: But you're an angel dear for swooping up our Andi

Cole: [eye roll emoji] ring a bell, I just earned my wings.

Jerome: [bell pepper emoji]

I caught up with Andi at baggage claim. They had earbuds in and weren't reading anything on their phone. Like, for example, the info about which sisters were already at the house, and who'd be spending only a few days with us.

No matter. We had the entire drive down to go over it.

On the rental car shuttle, they started typing, saying, "Jerome is going to love the confirmation."

"Confirmation?"

"Mm-hmm."

I couldn't see, since Andi tilted the phone deliberately away from me. "Confirmation of what? I know it's about me, after the literal novel he sent me about you."

They snort-laughed, which was barely cute at all. "I'm not surprised. And it's confirmation about your whole being in control kink."

"That's not my kink."

Andi started me down, and I tightened my jaw, refusing to break first. Or to blush, I hoped.

Their tiny, satisfied smile was practically a victory lap. "Noted. But even when you're trying to read over my shoulder, you can't help yourself. We're all the way in the back of this shuttle, but you keep leaning past me to check for oncoming traffic when the driver changes lanes. If that's not a need to control things—people, your environment—I don't know what it is."

I crossed my arms. "Jerome doesn't know all the things he thinks he knows."

"I have a spreadsheet with your sisters' shoe sizes on it that begs to differ."

It was hopefully too dark on the shuttle for any of the heat on my neck to give away my embarrassment. "In the past, people who've met the Dunways all at once have gotten overwhelmed. I didn't write all that up to quiz you on it, but this way, if you want any context, you'll have it."

Andi hummed as they stashed their phone in their backpack.

Once we'd made it onto a freeway headed south, I asked about the mushrooms. "Do you have any other dietary preferences? My sister texted that she'd put some basics in the beach cottage kitchen, but we can stop at a grocery if there's anything in particular you want. Or need."

"Your sister," they said, so flatly I couldn't tell if it was a question, a statement, or a poke at me.

I gave them a face value answer. "Emmeline."

"The youngest, right? Preparing for her master's degree, doesn't like crowds."

"It's not the people she minds. It's that her auditory processing disorder makes overlapping voices a pain in her ass."

"Yeah, I read the dossier."

I couldn't hold back my bark of laughter, even though their sarcasm at my expense was loud and clear. "Okay, Monarch of Misdirection—back to the food thing. Any allergies? Are you a coffee person? Tea? Soda? What do you like first thing in the morning?"

"Stop at that Whataburger at the next exit, and I'll let you learn by observing."

Person after my own heart. I did kinda revel in my new life in Philly, but there were very few taco trucks and not a single Whataburger. Nothing against Wawa, but no hoagie could compare to a jalapeño and cheese Whataburger. It was just facts.

They opted for the chicken sandwich and onion rings, both fully respectable choices, and offered to take over driving.

"I don't mind. Maybe once we get to Lake Jackson, that'll be about half the drive time."

Andi settled in, spending most of the drive typing away —I couldn't tell if it was texts or what. My own phone was buzzing at me, but it was hooked up to the rental's sound system, playing mostly villancicos and Tejano music. It's another fact that I have to listen to Selena while driving down the Gulf Coast, along the same roads that she traveled in her too-short life.

When she was murdered, I was barely a toddler, so her legacy has always been a part of my living memory. Falling for her music was, in that weird way that little kid brains work, a factor in my figuring out I was a boy. A lot of people assumed it was to do with seeing myself as different from all my sisters, and being the fourth of the six Dunways, I grew up witnessing plenty of iterations of girlhood. But for whatever reason—kid logic again—it was singing "Bidi Bidi Bom Bom" that I associated with the solid rightness of first naming my true self.

Andi didn't mention my music, but they bobbed their head and joined me in singing the chorus a couple of times. They didn't tell me any more about the family they weren't able to see this trip, or what other calumnies Jerome was spreading about me, or what they thought about the various things on my family agenda I'd sent.

So when one of Scorch's songs came up on my playlist and they lunged forward to turn it up and launched into a memorized-the-lyrics singalong, my heart rate spiked and I navigated us to the first safe place I could find to pull over.

FOUR

ANDI

"Um?"

Cole's hands flexed on the steering wheel as he stared at me.

"Did you need ..." I studied the strip center we were in. "Math tutoring?"

"You like Scorch Madigan?"

"You don't?" The song came from his playlist. I'd been smiling at another thing we had in common, to go with the long, erratic list Jerome kept amending. Two-thirds of it was just queer community monoculture, and I didn't believe Jerome knew how either Cole or I felt, specifically, about P-town or drag brunch.

Cole turned off the car and drew one of those deep 'I'm the most patient man to ever live' breaths of his. "You knew the stuff about Emmeline. So I thought you read my notes."

This again. "I did. There's also Jeannie, Larissa, Margo, and Sarita." I even knew them in alphabetical order.

His lips pressed together like I'd tested every single intact nerve he had. "And their spouses?"

Forgive me for not being over invested in the heteronormative institution of marriage. "All of them but Emmeline have partners. If I end up spending time with your family, I'm sure I'll sort out who's who."

His laugh was so raucous I was glad he'd pulled over. He couldn't seem to get out any words, and ended up gesticulating at my phone until I went ahead and pulled up his novel of an introduction to his family. It seemed like he wouldn't be satisfied otherwise.

The oldest sister, Larissa, was the one who still lived in Rockport. She and Alfie had two kids. Fine, good for them, whatever. And then I got to Jeannie and gulped a little. "Brendan Brody is your brother-in-law?" I couldn't yell at him about giving me a little heads-up, since he literally had, but I was itching to type a bunch of emojis at Jerome for leaving this off the stream of 'why I'll be fine spending Christmas with Cole' messages. Everyone knew Brendan Brody, Mr. Golden Throat himself, was pals with Scorch Madigan. They'd recorded a couple of songs for Scorch's last album—if Cole's playlist was that EP, one of their duets would have been the next up.

He squeezed his eyes together, pinching his brow. "Keep going."

I kept going. And then I stopped breathing.

When I could speak without screeching, I asked, "Sarita's husband. Ignatius?"

"Mmm." He pressed his lips together.

"Ignatius Madigan."

Cole nodded.

"Is also your brother-in-law?"

He nodded again.

I pointed at the now-silent radio. "Scorch Madigan is your brother-in-law."

Cole was snickering, and his hair did that flop over his

forehead thing that cast beguiling shadows over the sparkles in his eyes. I was bouncing between some kind of fury and some kind of glee, and my limbs all gave up on me. If any of the other Dunways were married to rock stars, I didn't have the strength to lift my phone and read about it.

"How did I not know this? Wait. Wait wait wait. Does *Jerome* not know this?"

Cole's head landed on the steering wheel as he belly-laughed. Eventually, he gasped back his amusement and said, "No one knows. A couple of people from work, cause I took them along to see Ignatius's concert stop right after I moved, but it turned into a whole mess. People intrusive enough we had to have a meeting about it, with HR and everything. So I stopped talking about them. But you'll meet Brendan and Ignatius both if you come to any of our events. I don't expect you to keep it a secret."

Right. Secrets. If I told our mutual friends about Cole's famous family members, the ones who knew my own secret would waste no time turning this into a Whole Deal. Not that my long-running space opera fic about Scorch, and all the drama that led up to him leaving his band for a solo career, was precisely a secret. Only something I didn't talk about with many people in meatspace.

So, no, letting Jerome know this detail wasn't happening. I didn't need anyone sending Cole all my AO3 links. It was bad enough, contemplating being under the same roof as Scorch for any part of the next couple of weeks. If it got back to Cole or his family that I wrote fan fiction featuring Scorch as a rogue starship captain leading her crew into danger throughout the Hyperion System, I'd need a black hole to absorb my embarrassment.

Sinking against the headrest, I summoned the will to really read the rest of Cole's dossier. No more major surprises, to my utter relief, but wow, did it seem like the Dunways were a lot of close-knit and fond of each other people. There were nicknames and inside jokes and gay uncles and cookie making parties. Actual Christmas cookie making and decorating and wrapping them in festive tins to distribute to friends and neighbors, like the most wholesome and loving intergenerational clan on the planet.

So. That was a lot.

Cole had himself under control, at least. I took over driving—opting against my usual road trip playlist with its heavy rotation of Scorch Madigan songs—and let him bang on about his life on the Gulf Coast as we moved out of Houston's almost endless suburban sprawl and into the abruptly wide spaces that would take us through to Rockport.

Since he wasn't quizzing me about my history, it wasn't the worst way to spend some time wrapping my mind around the unexpected changes to the way I'd anticipated coping with this holiday season.

CHAPTER
FIVE
COLE

I'd been texting the family all day, so they knew all about Andi needing to be rescued, and my plans to share the cottage with them. I'd gotten a couple of sarcastic emojis and unnecessary memes—outside the group text with all the elders, thank God—and plenty of assurances that they'd be as hospitable to Andi as they'd want.

Still, I hadn't expected the welcome party as we pulled up.

I'd directed Andi straight to the cottage, figuring they'd want the option to settle in after the disruptions of their day. But since Aunt Max and two of my sisters were sitting on the loungers on the porch, it seemed like they wouldn't get the option.

"So that's my parents' best friend Maxima, we call her Aunt Max. And Emmeline and Gogo. Margo, I mean."

"The younger sisters."

I was starting to enjoy that exasperated tone of Andi's. They were clearly making up for having glossed over my family tree earlier, by acting like all the info I provided was excessive. Pretending they hadn't been legit shaken up by the truth of my famous brothers-in-law.

I desperately wanted to tell Gogo all about it, but I'd have to wait until this trip was all over. It would likely piss Andi off, if they thought I was making light of their being star-struck. Besides, a random bit of gossip wasn't near as important to me as barreling into the arms of the family I hadn't seen in so long.

I shot Andi my most reassuring smile. Because even though they clearly didn't believe it yet, they were gonna love the Dunways. Everyone loved the Dunways—it was like our family motto. They made a shooing motion I barely caught in my periphery as I hustled up to meet everyone on the walkway.

"Gogo, what's with your unexpected arrival? I thought you and Karl were due to come in with Sarita?" I asked Margo. My closest sister. I utterly loved all of them, but Margo was the one I'd roomed with for years during college and just after, including the pandemic years. Even though I lived in Philly now, and she lived mostly on the road while managing Scorch, our bubble would never burst.

"But you're forgetting how good I am at my job," Margo said, squeezing me back. "I got him all set up for the Dallas shows and we hightailed it out of there. I had to get back to see my—"

"Your favorite brother. Of course."

She swatted my shoulder. "My only brother."

"And always your fave."

"To see who my only brother is bringing home to meet the family."

Emmeline—who was, of all gorgeous, generous, Gen Z things, wearing a she/her pronoun pin—raised a hand. "Ditto."

I smothered her in my next hug. "Don't even. It's not like that."

After kissing Aunt Max on each cheek, I added, "I mean it. There's nothing to read into here. I know you all have unsubtle minds, but this is just me helping out a friend. They were in a situation and I could help, so I did. I don't want y'all doing anything to make them uncomfortable. They're already ..."

"I'm already what?" Andi spoke up from behind me. Their voice was mild; their expression wasn't.

I reached for their suitcase and tucked it up by the cottage door. "Already having to deal with me and my opinionated, controlling ways, apparently."

"Wait, who said that? Did you say that?" Margo turned to Andi. "I love you for saying that. Please keep telling Cole how no one likes it when he's Bossy McBosserton."

I crossed my arms and narrowed my eyes at my sister. "They didn't say they didn't like it."

"I don't like it when you're Bossy McBosserton, Cole." At least Andi seemed to have rediscovered their wry humor, even if it was at my expense.

Emmeline returned from the car with the rest of our luggage. "Thanks, sweet pea. It's a joy to be welcomed home by someone so thoughtful and generous."

Emmers shouldered me aside as I went to help her bring everything inside. "You're hardly going to impress them by being a total brat."

"I'm not trying to impress them," I hissed, like that would make my words less likely for Andi to overhear.

Emmeline's look was far from convinced. I turned to Aunt Max. "Good to see you, as always, but can I ask why I'm seeing you at this particular moment?" She patted my cheek, which I knew from experience was a step from turning into a hair ruffle if I didn't duck away fast.

"I heard about your friend coming in and came to make the offer that Margo rejected last year. I've got that apartment above the garage. My Luis is staying there, but if you need extra accommodation, he's got room, and we've got a spare bed frame in the garage. Although ..." She looked pointedly between me and the possibly defensive way I was shielding Andi from her. "It looks like you're not interested in taking me up on it."

SIX

ANDI

I followed the youngest Dunway into the cottage, more than ready to escape the atmosphere of teasing nonsense that seemed to delight everyone outside. It's not like Cole was the only person I knew with a family all up in each other's business. More power to those with families of origin full of unconditional love; the world needed plenty of that.

My only objection was being unwillingly placed in the role of appreciative audience member to their teasing antics. It wasn't my job to catalog and appreciate them all enjoying each other's company.

So I escaped inside. The cottage was both about what I'd expected, and better than I'd feared. Something about the way Cole had described it—an overflow property at the end of his family land—had left me wincing with reflexive anti-rich people vibes. One of the side effects of growing up where I had, among the big brick houses and planned communities that were a hallmark of Houston's economy. Not that my parents hadn't been a part of all that, or that I hadn't received direct material advantages because of it. But those advantages never meant I wasn't subjected to the conservative values and dismissive attitudes that tended to go along with them.

Hence, my stepmother's dictates and the fact that I was here at all, appreciating that the cottage was well-built but not high end, and comfortable without kitschiness.

Ignoring the apparently comfortable sofa, I took my backpack through the door beside the tidy little kitchen and discovered the bedroom. It wasn't exactly small, but with a queen bed dominating most of the space, I wouldn't have a lot of room to pace around, not without being in the Cole-occupied part of the cottage.

Or on the beach beyond.

I left my bag and coat on the bed, only pulling out my yellow and purple scarf to wrap around myself if the ocean breezes bothered me. I preferred the feeling of staying bundled up in my awesome sweaters and coats all the long winter that came with life in Philly, but here I was in a place that was warm, even in winter. Kind of like hell, but Texas, instead.

I emerged to an empty cottage, all the nonsense seemingly still contained on the front porch. All the family members gave me sneaking out of the house vibes when I took off through the kitchen door. The property wasn't fenced, and, as promised, the sand was steps away. I followed a boardwalk past a series of dunes until the noise of the humanity faded in favor of wind and waves and seabirds.

We were near a major refuge for migratory birds. Cole's dossier mentioned that both his uncle and the godmother they all called Aunt Max were involved in the tourism industry that centered on the overwintering flocks. The further I walked along the shore, the more in sympathy with those birds I felt, despite the strange unseasonable heat and how all the river sediment flowing into the Gulf always left the water brown in a way that reminded me of the proliferation of offshore rigs.

Still, there was something peaceful and soul settling about this stretch of coastline. The hum of the waves and the steady rhythm of my steps on the hard packed sand. I even found myself humming as I walked back to the cottage.

The sight of Cole lounging at his ease against the porch railing as I approached clicked some puzzle pieces into place. *Sun faded lounge chair / Gulls crying overhead /Mind skipping, tripping, flipping me / Saying things I shouldn't have said.* It was a Scorch Madigan song crowding into my subconscious.

I stopped short at the possibly iconic porch, meeting Cole's questioning look with one of my own. "This is where Scorch wrote 'Sunspots,' isn't it?"

And like that, I had Cole laughing. "Sarita is going to love the hell out of you."

"I'll take that as a yes."

He spread his arms, acting like the cottage—like his whole life—was an exhibit I'd come to study at my leisure. Like I wasn't one step up from stranded, and never mind the odds I'd meet some musicians I enjoyed. They weren't the reason I'd been trapped in Texas.

Maybe my expression revealed some of that lonely bitterness that had followed me south like my own personal migratory flock of feelings. Cole straightened, swallowing, and scratched at that bright-dark beard of his. "You good?"

"Sure, why wouldn't I be?"

His nod took me at my word, leaving me to wonder why such serene acceptance felt instead like a judgment.

CHAPTER

SEVEN

COLE

When we caught sight of Andi walking down to the beach, I'd done my best to cut short the rampant, misguided speculation about our relationship.

Aunt Max kept harping on about me staying at her place, ignoring that I'd never got round to actually liking her son. I wasn't set on blaming the guy for the laughter and ignorant things he'd said, back when he was fifteen and I was twelve, and I'd finally told everybody else I was a boy.

I hadn't really considered, before opening my mouth, that I would be the first trans person in the lives of most people I knew. Even with my family as a buffer, I'd fielded more vicious comments than anything Luis had spouted. In retrospect, my younger self had had a lot of unearned, but essential, bravado. But after Luis and Sarita's high school attempts to date had smashed into the rocks, she wasn't the only one happy enough to let him drift out of our daily lives.

Aunt Max was more than worth the bore of having him

around, though I still didn't want to stay at her house. "I'm not leaving Andi sequestered here by themself, not when I'm the only person they even know in Rockport. That's not in the Christmas spirit at all."

"And sharing the cottage with them for a week and a half is, what, the top thing on their holiday wishlist?"

I pointed at Margo. "Don't start making up stories. I told you we're just friends. Barely even that, since the drive down was the first time we've talked for more than two or three minutes at a time."

"Has he always looked at all of his friends like that, or just since moving to Philly?" Emmeline asked Margo.

"Know what? You two are my baby sisters. It's against the rules for you to tease me this much. Go away and come back when you can show me a proper amount of deference and respect."

Max's eyebrows bounced with laughter. "And what about me, young man? Am I old enough to tease you?"

"I have all the respect for you, Maxima, but I know you're too gracious and kind-hearted to make me feel self conscious. Do you know what I really want us all to do? Help Andi feel comfortable staying here, and maybe even give them a really fun holiday to counteract a bit of the bullshit from their family."

Since I'd gone and made myself emotional and intro-spective talking to them, I thanked everyone for setting up the cottage for us and told them I'd meet them up at the house later.

When Andi returned, I guided them on a tour of the cottage. Not that it needed much explication. The whole thing was a tad bigger than a typical mid-priced hotel suite, but, crucially, the only way into the bathroom was through

Andi's room. "If you're comfortable with the bedroom staying unlocked overnight, I've got this screen Max probably found in her garage—sorry, family joke, Max's garage overflows with all the spare furniture you need for any occasion. So. The screen. We can use it to make a little corridor for me to use and hopefully not disturb you much?"

My hesitant words made my stomach tight. I'd arranged for the screen and all the other amenities the family had rounded up during our trip down from Philly, but I was speaking conditionally. As if I hadn't already figured out how to make the cottage work for us to share.

Andi folded out the panels, standing back to consider the view from the bathroom doorway. "Thanks?"

Okay, it was a rattan screen, and not exactly opaque. But Max hadn't told me that when she volunteered it.

I hauled a spare sheet from the closet and draped it across the screen. "There, now. I have granted you invisibility."

The grin Andi flashed at me felt like it was more at something internal than at my dad joke-tier humor.

"That's all I've ever wanted." Their affect lightened considerably, and for the first time, I really got what Jerome had been saying about them.

I cleared my throat. "Right. So. That's the whole place. And you already found the beach path."

"It's nice. The boardwalk and all. Peaceful."

Now my affect was the one chilling out. I backed to the main room, giving them plenty of space, and myself a little plausible deniability about any blushing.

"I'm just gonna check on the bedding for the sofa." I launched into an explanation of Emmeline bringing over blankets and a sleep mask for me, and how the morning sun streamed in from the main windows, before I cut myself off.

They didn't need a play-by-play of how to make up a bed. They could see everything I was doing, and I doubted my transparency ended there.

I dug out my phone to check the time, swallowing my thoughts about how many messages had piled up. Seemed like everyone I'd ever met was taking the chance to gossip in my absence.

"Right. Dinner is up at the house in about two hours. You're welcome to join us."

They were hovering in the bedroom doorway and shaking their head. "I'll stay here. It's ... been a day. Plus, I'm still full of Whataburger. But thank you. You've very much gone out of your way to help, and it's a big deal to me."

If we got into a war of politeness, Jerome would fall down making fun of us both. And I wanted to be further down the road to relaxed friendship with Andi. Not, as I was sure the messages from Jerome and Liz and Sybil claimed, because of the one measly time I sloppily hinted at crushing on Andi.

It would just make the trip home easier for all of us if Andi didn't constantly feel the need to be gracious.

My own feelings didn't come into it.

CHAPTER

EIGHT

ANDI

I didn't always read faces well, but Cole'd had this look when I encouraged him, for the nineteenth time, to go ahead to his family, instead of waiting until dinner time to leave me alone.

It was maybe a tad wistful? Longing?

I was making things up. I'd been suckered into liking him a little, and now my brain had these hyperbolic ideas about fitting in and being not just a holiday anomaly, but somehow part of things. It had no basis for concocting those kinds of fantasies.

The real problem boiled down to that screen.

It must have occurred to Cole that my sharing a cottage with him for a week and a half meant ten full days of his company. Being seen, morning, noon, and night.

At least at my stepmother's, I'd have been able to retreat to a room of my own. And I'd have spent more time with my half-sisters than with anyone else, anyway. The girls didn't see me as an oddity. It was just a given that I preferred to 'play dress up' my way. Not with their frothy

29

princess gowns and shiny pink capes, but with my dyed undercuts and graphic button-downs.

They didn't question it, even while their mother used their schooling as a reason to forbid me from using my preferred pronouns. It was one of the things our father had bargained with me about: I'd let the misgendering stand until the girls were ten, and he'd then insist that the family could use they/them without it messing up their English grades.

But he was gone now, and Evelyn was not holding to any of her dead husband's promises.

So, of all the things I'd braced for encountering at Evelyn's house, I had at least left on this trip expecting to have hours with a door between me and anyone who refused to respect the full range of my personhood.

Jerome had sent me reams of texts vouching for Cole, and he was, to all appearances, a solid member of my community. But he wasn't someone I actually knew well. Yes, he'd scooped me up with every appearance of kindness, and even with an attempt to rein in his obvious hero complex. But the enthusiasm and specificity of his hard sell of the Dunway family Christmas left me itching with the sense that I'd be performing happy guest mode as relentlessly as I'd have been battling against gender essentialism at Evelyn's.

And then he'd arranged for that screen for the bedroom, and conjured up the obscuring sheet. And said it guaranteed my invisibility, like he already understood my need to sometimes exist in space, without wondering what anybody thought of my appearance.

Like, even on the journey down, while he was being subjected to his own barrage of texts from Jerome, he'd made space to think about my specific desires. To let my needs influence his actions. It was damn thoughtful, and drenched me in a sensation I never expected to encounter again within Texas' borders. That of being throughly understood, and seen in a way that went so much further than skin deep.

So yeah, I needed more time alone than just that short walk on the beach had given me. I needed time to settle into the odd reality of the situation.

The whole day was messing with my head. I'd woken up early to get to the airport, and sat there with my sad overpriced muffin and fairly decent coffee, journaling to get in a headspace that would let me show up at Evelyn's, ready to focus on my sisters. It was only our third holiday without Dad, and I was determined to keep alive some of the holiday traditions we'd grown up with.

As much as we'd had the occasional problem as I'd aged into knowing myself as an individual outside the family unit, and as much as Evelyn tried to override some of our traditions with some of hers even before the girls had come along, Dad had always loved making the holiday season exciting for me.

So I had all these ideas for us. Going to the mall ice rink to try to skate. Driving through some of the extravagant neighborhoods to see the fancy light displays. Cutting dozens and dozens of paper snowflakes. I'd gotten to where I was really looking forward to the visit. Especially me and Dad's favorite: building a blanket fort I'd sleep in after we watched *The Muppet Christmas Carol.*

So when I texted Evelyn with my flight status update, I barely even flinched when instead of her usual thumbs up emoji, she phoned me. And told me her dictates, should I opt to spend the holiday with my sisters.

And that's how Cole found me hunched and pacing at

our gate, trying to sort out how to establish myself in Evelyn's house, when she'd installed a man with even less respect for who I was than she had, and neither had any intention of honoring the wishes of the father my sisters and I had lost.

NINE

COLE

My parents' house was a party even before their annual holiday party got underway. Being the fourth of six kids, I'd grown up with a reasonable tolerance for chaos, but our gatherings had exploded in recent years. For the longest time, only my oldest sister was married, but now everyone else but Emmeline was partnered, and Larissa had two kids. I was impressed by how baby Spencer, currently cradled in my arms and not going anywhere if I had anything to say about it, stayed calm while his aunts, uncles, and grands tried their best to tease me.

"Haven't you ever seen Cole with a crush?" Margo asked Emmeline. "He goes all protective and turns into their brand manager. 'Did you know this person has a strong sense of global responsibility? Have I told you about that person's elegant taste? You've never met anyone as compassionate as her!' And on and on, like a new press release every day."

"Your impression of me is spot on."

Gogo just laughed at me, adding insult to insult by trying to snatch away the baby.

"Hey, back off. Spencer only loves people who don't make fun of his favorite uncle."

"I didn't make fun of you. I explained your whole hype man persona, is all."

"And who says I have a crush on Andi, anyway?" Oops to me, since my voice went all petulant at the question. I focused on Spencer's cute nommy cheeks and his baby thing of having wrist wrinkles, instead of any of the three sisters in the room.

"Me." That was Emmeline, blunt as always.

Ignoring the chorus of assent, I took Spencer into the living room so I could chat with Larissa's other kid, too. Alfie launched into an explanation of every piece of his wood puzzle for me, identifying most of the animals and all the colors correctly. It was a lot more fun than sitting around the dining table with Larissa, Alfie Sr., Margo, Karl, and Emmeline as they told me what they thought was my business.

Never mind that time I mentioned to Liz and Sybil how I thought Andi was attractive and I admired how they used their sharp observational skills to foster connections between people. My sisters didn't know about that.

Mama and Dad came in and bracketed me on the sofa. "How are you, hijo?"

It made me smile, like always, when Mama called me 'son' in Spanish. We grew up speaking casual Spanish, mostly to do with home tasks and the music that over-flowed each room of the house until we knew how that messed with Emmeline's auditory processing disorder. But almost as soon as I told my parents I was a boy, Mama stopped saying, "Bueno, hijas mías, lávense," in favor of, "Niños, cepillaos los dientes."

That's who they were. They modeled to all of us that our emotional and psychological needs were as important as our physical ones.

"Isn't he perfect?" I leaned into Dad so he could get a better gander at Spencer's face.

"He looks like you did when you were born."

And there went my breath. I couldn't look away from my nephew's slanting eyebrows and tuft of dark hair. It was one thing to see so much Dunway in him; the family resemblance was strong with all of us. But hell if it didn't hit me in a particular spot I never knew my soul possessed, to hear this infant boy took after his only blood-relative uncle. "He does?"

"Most definitely. You had those same jowls."

"And the round eyes," Mama added, her voice a smile. "Only you and your dad have those eyes. The girls are all almond-shaped, like me."

"Am my eyes almonds, Buela?"

Mama scooped up Alfie and pretended to taste his features, naming each one a different nut. As they tumbled off the sofa to continue the game, Dad anchored me to his side, so I didn't jostle Spencer. "After six babies, we got good at identifying individual features. Especially before everything was digitally date-stamped. You kids all looked too much the same for us to tell at a glance which baby picture was whose. You and Larissa with the jowls, but her eyes are like Carmen's. Jeannie's face is the most heart-shaped, but Emmeline and Sarita are nearly the same."

"Did Sarita always have the curls?"

"No, but her hair was always the lightest. And not thick like our Spencer here."

I let Dad pry the baby from my arms and went to study the framed studio portraits on the wall. The first couple, of Larissa and Jeannie, were from exactly their six-month birthdays. The rest of us were from sometime between five and eight months old. Each of us was wearing blue overalls, presumably the same pair passed down, and various onesies underneath. Mine was yellow with purple polka-dots; I'd studied it for a while when I was twelve and Dad walked me through the various pictures on display in the house so I could choose which to take down.

I hadn't compared my image to those of my sisters, not really. Active 1: I had internalized our similarities enough that I was surprised when I noticed a cousin's baby picture and realized that not every baby looks like a Dunway baby. But looking now, I got Dad's point about our slightly distinct features.

And, yeah. Of all six Dunway babies on that wall, the one Spencer looked most like was me.

CHAPTER
TEN

ANDI

Cole sang all the way up the path to the porch, so it wasn't surprising when he burst back into the cottage. I still jumped and slammed my laptop shut.

Not that he seemed to notice, busy as he was setting a covered plate on the breakfast bar, and babbling about his family again.

I studied the dossier he gave me. I'd even searched out recent photos of Scorch Madigan and Brendan Brody to catch sight of them with Cole's sisters—the ones they were married to, and also Margo, who worked for Scorch. And it surprised me how little gossip there was about both singers marrying into the not-fame-adjacent Dunway family.

Much as I liked Scorch's music, in particular, I'd never paid much attention to his personal life. I'd been inspired by the speculation when he'd left The Evil Stepbrothers, but at this point my fic had very little to do with Scorch or anyone's public persona.

I shoved my laptop aside as Cole flopped down beside

me. "The chicken's still hot, I think. It's got a rosemary and balsamic glaze."

"Sounds great, thanks."

"It is great. And tomorrow, after we kayak, we were talking about going for tacos."

"You kayak?"

He gave a little bounce. "Yep, in the Bay. It's supposed to be sunny tomorrow, but we've got wind protection stuff you can borrow, and water shoes, and life vests, of course."

"Since when am I kayaking?"

His eyes were bright as the bulbs strung on the mini Christmas tree in the living room's corner. "It's so great. The water, the fish darting past your paddle, all the birds scoping us out. You get this exhilarated feeling at the same time you're settling into such a peaceful state. It's entirely transporting."

"Until I fall in."

"I'd never let that happen. I've been paddling since I was tiny, and we'll be in tandem boats. It'll be too late in the day for the dolphins, probably, but when you love it, we can see about finding another time to catch them."

I wasn't reassured. "You're very enthusiastic."

He grinned and hopped up, reaching a hand to pull me to my feet. "Come eat. I'm going to have a beer; want one?"

"Only if it's the IPA." I'd snooped through the fridge earlier; Cole's family had stocked the kitchen with more food than I imagined the two of us needing for the next ten days. But he'd brought me a plate from his family table, anyway.

And held my hand longer than I'd expected, leading me the few steps from the sofa to the counter.

"Hey, I didn't ask. Did you get on okay while I was gone?"

Unwrapping the foil from my dinner, I nodded. "Unpacked, got online, all good." I didn't mention the knot in my gut I got separating my clothes from my half-sisters' gifts. I'd bundled Estella's and Cassiopeia's presents in the shirts I'd hoped would be femme enough to pass Evelyn's muster.

Not that my normal attire was all masc. I wore clothing from across a spectrum, because some days I found comfort for myself in softer looks, and some days I needed edges. Because, for me, the social expression of my being nonbinary was full of variety, and full of what brings me joy.

It was something I'd never quite articulated growing up. Never had to, not when my dad let me pick whatever I wanted to wear and only cared if I put away my laundry promptly. And then, when I was fourteen, he married Evelyn.

She decided my autonomy over my clothing choices arose from Dad's lax single parenting, and began subjecting me to her version of what was right for me to wear. I'd spent years piecing together outfits from what she bought, and what I could sneak out of Dad's closet to cover over all the figure-hugging floral shit. It wasn't easy, even on the mornings he suggested she let me be, to go through the daily gauntlet of her inspection.

It did give me clear information on what she'd say about every boxy shirt and straight-leg pant I packed for this trip. Even the ones in softer colors. Even my favorite button-down with the black and white bird motif. They were all items I'd worn regularly, but the thing was, I'd left behind the parts of my wardrobe I normally used to make these more Evelyn-acceptable pieces fit the Andi I truly was.

So separating out my clothes left me all too aware of the

ways I'd imposed limits on my self-expression. It wasn't like it mattered if anyone in Cole's family judged me; I'd leave Rockport soon enough. And if the tradeoff was more meals like this chicken dish, it wouldn't even be too painful to wait out Christmas with the Dunways—not even the one who was rambling about his sister's kids and showing off the photos taken during the few hours we've been apart.

"Okay, so Alfie is a total chatterbox, which he does not get from his father, by the way. Anyone who gets two sentences out of Alfie Senior earns an entry in the Senior Speaks Sweepstakes."

"The what?"

"It's okay, he's in on it. He's the one who certifies each entry. Larissa isn't allowed to play, so she holds the pot. It's five bucks a person—I'll spot you if you're in. Oh, and it doesn't count if he's talking to his kids. But that's what I wanted to show you. Look. Okay, this is baby Spencer."

I looked. It was a baby.

"He was four months old last week. So he's in that whole sturdy neck, nosy about everything phase. But look at this."

The next photo was also the baby, but closer up this time. "Cute."

"So cute. The cutest. And look." Cole swiped to the next pic, which of a framed baby photo, one of those portrait studio things with oversized blocks in the background. "Mama and Dad were pointing out how much he looks like me. That's me at six months, and then checkout Spencer."

He was swiping back and forth so fast I hardly had time to draw comparisons. But his voice had cracked enough that I sat down my cutlery and paid attention. "Slow down."

Cole placed the phone in my hands like it was as fragile

as the baby he was showing me, and like I'd released a spring, he started pacing. "It's just, my whole life, no matter how long or short my hair. Or if I was the only one not wearing makeup. Or anything. It was always, 'Those Dunways are such peas in a pod.' We're all just clones of Mama. And I know that's about more than gender. I can look at pictures of any of us before puberty, and it's hard to tell who's who. I can't say that never gave me a sense of belonging—I'm sure it did, but ..."

He took back the phone and stared at the picture of him holding the baby. "We all look like Mama. And so much of her side of the family is women. Aunts, cousins, sisters." He swiped again, coming to rest on a picture of him, the baby and toddler, and an older man who must have been his father.

"Until today I never could have guessed how affirming it would be to have somebody say, 'This baby boy looks just like you.'"

CHAPTER
ELEVEN
COLE

"You get all that?"

Andi nodded, and I allowed myself one more visual inspection before accepting they were ready. We'd had a quiet morning, Andi heading off for a solo beach walk while I helped Emmers create a grad school application spreadsheet. I didn't know if that was because I'd made them uncomfortable the evening before, or if having me sleep on the sofa in the next room had been weird for them, or if they were just not much for mornings.

But when Margo and Karl had swung by with the kayaks, Andi perked up and got chatty, asking them on the way to the marina about the black mangroves and various sea grasses we'd encounter on the paddling trails. The sea was a little rougher and the air a little cooler than forecasted, so we'd opted to go to the sloughs on Redfish Bay, rather than the open water to St Jo's Island.

All the way across the Aransas Pass, Andi engaged as if our local ecology entranced them. And now it was just the two of us going over my brief paddling instructions, they withdrew. Maybe I was over-analyzing, on edge because I'd overshared the day before. I'd gotten used to sharing things like that with my queer friends, but that didn't mean Andi was up for hearing my confessions. Even if they seemed to take it in stride at the time.

Karl called a question to us. I caught the moment Andi's cheek lifted in a friendly crease before turning to wave at him. "Right behind you."

It was the same affable look they'd had the first time I'd met them. Jerome had indulged my questions about Andi when I pulled him aside, even the ones I hadn't asked. Like, do they date, and if so, are trans men part of their dating pool?

Yes, and probably, for the record.

Their almost defensive facade of friendliness stopped me from getting blatant about my attraction back at home. It was a relief to see them drop it before me, in favor of truer emotions like aggravation, frustration, and even a bit of desperation, since running into them at the airport.

But that relief was tempered by the knowledge that Andi was stuck with me for the next week or so. I wouldn't put them in the position of needing their armor around me again.

At the launch spot, Margo and Karl checked for oncoming craft in the Aransas Channel, then took off in their own kayak. After Andi sat, I handed them their paddle and hopped in behind, pushing us off. As I slid into place, matching their pace, we crossed the channel and followed my sister into Cutters Loop.

It took Andi only a few minutes to get the hang of paddling. Their stiff posture relaxed, and their grip on the paddle softened as we moved into the mangroves. They watched the way Margo and Karl maneuvered their boat and settled into a steady rhythm, which increased as we approached the others.

I liked how they trusted me to match their strokes. To steer and to navigate and to keep us secure.

Margo glanced over her shoulder as we approached, and gave me the raised eyebrows that meant, "Hey, you brought a ringer along?"

My expression was smug as we shot past her, and then all four of us were laughing as we raced over the gentle, shallow water, and deeper into the marshy maze. Margo and Karl won, but only because Andi lost their rhythm when a bird hop-flapped away from us and into the gnarled roots of the mangroves to our left.

They swung around to gape at it. "What's that?"

"Great Blue Heron," I said. "There's another in that cutaway. See that? Looks like some rough rocks just under the water? That's an oyster bed. It's a tasty place for the birds to hang. If the water was clearer today, we'd see some crabs around here, too, and all kinds of fish. It's why so many species of birds overwinter down here."

As I pointed, I spotted Karl taking our photo. He waved. "Doing okay back there?"

Andi shot me a grin over their shoulder, and I sucked in my breath at the way the water lent silver to the gray of their eyes. And I exhaled slowly, because it wasn't my goal for my houseguest to guess at my horny thoughts.

They didn't act like they were anything but casually pleased to be near me. "I admit you were right. I love this."

"Hope you still feel that way by the time we get to dinner. Don't forget to take a break when you need one. Your shoulders aren't used to this."

"You calling me a wimp?"

"I would never sell your strength short. It's only my

experience of picking up a paddle after too long away, and we've got another hour at least before we're back to the car."

They gave me a solid nod and turned back to the prow of the kayak. "Let's see some more birds and stuff, then, and make the ache worth it."

CHAPTER

TWELVE

ANDI

We sped our boats back across the channel and settled into Margo's car, leaving me a little salt-sprayed and a little damp-legged and a little sandy between my toes.

And a little more pleased than I'd thought this excursion would render me.

Cole, of course, was back to vibrating with his usual high-frequency happiness. That calm he'd promised from being out on the water hadn't lasted long. "Tacos. Tacos, Andi? Karl?" He drummed his hands on his sister's headrest. "Gogo, we want tacos. Fish tacos. Let's go to that place out by Karl's old church. No, wait. Is the one by the marina still open, you think?"

"They moved to that strip center off Market. Anyway, we're not going there. We're going onto the island."

"Oh, sweet." He went on about Mustang Island, and how there used to be wild horses there, and how he always thought if he hung out by the sea oats that grew near our cottage, he might catch sight of one of now-gone equines, and how the migratory cranes would chase him away from their overwintering hangouts.

"You really like it here."

That drew him up short. "I mean. Yeah? It's home."

My face might have alerted him. Or maybe it was three seconds of consideration for the way the state had its foot on the necks of women and queer people.

"Okay, I know it's imperfect as hell. I didn't leave just because of a great job offer."

Margo reached back and squeezed his knee. He held her hand a sec before letting her put it back on the wheel. "Obviously I'm lucky. I had the family's support, and back when I was eighteen, it was nerve-wracking but not actively dangerous, fixing my legal status. Small town connections actually helped—our doctor knew I was Cole for years. Our cousin works at the courthouse and pointed me to the right judge to bring my petition to. Plus, my Uncle Bill—you'll meet him tonight, if you come to dinner with us. He gave me a job so I could repay my top surgery."

"And so you could get buff hauling laundry around," Margo added.

"Every boy new to T should get a gig cleaning hotel rooms." Cole showed off his arms, like no one had ever noticed the way he kept fit. Like his muscles didn't always flex and shift under his shirts. "Point is, a decade ago, all those things lined up for me—with time, with support, but I got here. If I was doing them today, it wouldn't go so well. Which is one reason I live in Philly now, even though it means missing my family. And missing these barrier islands, and the warm winters, and decent Mexican food."

We'd made it to the cantina, which put a halt to Cole's paean to his hometown. Which was just as well, because his enthusiasm for the place was striking a false note.

I didn't doubt his feelings for his family. But his determination to focus on the best of the place ignored or discounted that he, as someone who now conformed to a gender norm, could move through this part of the world without having to navigate some things I did.

Things like the look I got from the mom at the changing table, when I opted for the women's restroom at the restaurant. I always chose the women's room, when a single stall or all-gender space wasn't an option. But sometimes—like when I was stuck in the state where I first had to learn to articulate my thoughts about my gender, or when I was spending time with someone actively reveling in how he'd dispatched the legal and social barriers to claiming his manhood—the fact of having to pick where to pee rankled to the depths of my nonconforming soul.

It wasn't so much too long for, was it? The ability to move through the world without having to explain myself?

I let down my topknot and cocked my hip and pasted on a smile as I washed the ocean off my hands. The mom smiled back as she secured her baby in the stroller and cleaned herself up. I held the door for them to exit ahead of me, and she thanked me, and I didn't drop my facade until I'd slid into the booth beside Cole.

"You good?" He slid my drink over.

"Mm." Which wasn't an answer, so I decapitated the straw wrapper and pointed the straw at him. "This is for splashing me."

He reared back as much as he could, but my weaponized tube of paper flew the few inches to bop him on the cheek. "It was a total accident. I was steering us away from that bed of seagrass. They're protected, you know."

"I think they can survive being gently displaced by a

shallow boat. That one fishing person was practically thrashing in their clump to net that trout or whatever it was."

"Redfish, probably," Margo said. "But Andi's right, as long as we're not in there with propellers, the seagrass is fine. You didn't need to splash them."

Karl draped an arm around Margo. "Interesting statement in defense of the splash-ee there, my love."

Her side-eye left us all chuckling as our server delivered dinner, and I spun the good mood out with questions about the environmental impact of fishing boats on the barrier islands. It related enough to my job that I could chat easily without showing off the bruises on my soul.

That, and some truly tasty fare, got us through the outing and on our way back to the solitude of the cottage.

THIRTEEN

I knew how to read a room, even when that room was my sister's car. I let Andi be, other than hoping they enjoyed the info I pumped Margo and Karl for about Scorch's current tour. Margo'd been Scorch's PA for about as long as I'd been in Philly. Before that, we'd shared an apartment in Austin for most of our adult lives, so I knew well that we turned into a jumble of in jokes and shorthand whenever we hung out. Karl was mostly adjusted to our nonsense. And since he'd spent plenty of time hanging out with Ignatius and Sarita, as he took his own work on the road to be with Margo, I was facing the unwelcome new reality of being an outsider in her life.

So, that was a harsh reminder to be an adult about our banter, and not leave Andi constantly playing catch-up.

Not that they acted like they felt excluded. They did that thing again, where they were engaged with everything without injecting themself into anything. Jerome had called it the "Andi is everyone's friend equally syndrome," but— and I'd never question his labels to his face, as that way lay barbed dragons—I was sensing some nuance Jerome never mentioned. It wasn't simply that Andi had that chameleon way of getting along with all the people.

They also used it to keep their shields up.

I'd always liked Andi, because they made sure everyone did. But I kept glimpsing a core that was a good deal more raw, and even more appealing for that realness. That was the Andi I wanted to be allowed to like.

After breakfast and another beach walk with coffee the next morning, I hung outside, giving Andi the first crack at the shower while the rising sun pierced the shadows of the porch. Later, emerging from my shower, I almost bumped into them pacing the bedroom, using their calm voice on the phone.

"I know that. I'm not trying to bypass your rules, Evelyn. If I was, I wouldn't be calling first. But they're my sisters, and I'm in Texas, and ..."

I palmed their shoulder blade to move by, and was startled when Andi leaned into my touch. They pivoted, letting me see their furrowed brow and tight eyes, before wrapping their free arm around me and resting their head on my shoulder.

My damp from the shower, towel draped, otherwise bare shoulder. My own arm cradled them, stroking their upper arm as they listened to their stepmother lay down, from what I could tell, all kinds of dictates. Not the ideal time to be considering how Andi's warmth and the alchemy of their scent with the cottage bath products and the way they made me laugh all combined to build a constant yearning in my boxers.

So I kept my eyes off their curves, and their muscles, and their fancy rainbow dyed undercut. Instead, I spotted two near-identical gift boxes on the bed, and a jumble of other wrapped items in Andi's open suitcase. The boxes, wrapped in sparkly winter paper and tied up with snowflake-embossed tulle, screamed "special gifts for my little sisters."

They must have taken up a good third of Andi's checked bag.

"Right. Yeah. I get it. Okay. Bye."

Even more of Andi's weight came to rest against me as they hung up. I nestled them closer, letting my pec serve as a pillow for their forehead and ignoring the trail of their resigned sigh across my chest. "Into talking about it?"

They shook their head.

I held them, quiet. Eventually, they gave a forced little laugh and pressed away. Which meant I also ignored their palms on my ribs, because I was stoic like that.

Ha.

"Sorry, didn't mean to waylay you on your way to get dressed."

Ha, again. I searched for a reply that didn't reveal how much I didn't mind being undressed around them. "It's no problem. Waylay me whenever you need."

They laughed like I wasn't sincere. Or like my sincerity wasn't important to them. But they also patted at my chest and ducked their head like they were hiding a blush, which only puffed me up more.

"So. That was your stepmother."

Andi's sigh sank into me, smothering my mood. "Yeah."

I tilted my head in invitation, and they followed me into the living room. I grabbed for my jeans because it seemed like I should cover my ass if we were going to talk seriously. "And those presents?"

"For Estella and Cassiopeia." They sat on the sofa and tossed over the clean shirt I'd laid out there. "I have a few other gifts, things I was going to bring to this thing with

Evelyn's family we always—they always, I mean—have on the twenty-third. While we were at dinner, I realized one of them would maybe be nice for Margo. So then I was going to go through and see what else I can give to people here, you know?"

I fell to the cushion beside them. "That's so damn nice. You don't have to give us anything."

Andi's huff of laughter wasn't overflowing with humor. "Evelyn didn't drum every one of her opinions into my head, but host gifts seem like a good one to hold on to. Besides, they're nothing much. Some scarves, a travel scrapbook—that's what I thought Margo would like."

"She absolutely will. You're going to make me up my gift game to compete."

Now Andi's smile was genuine. "I am, indeed, notoriously hard to beat."

"Challenge accepted."

I wrapped my arm around them, and their head came to rest on my shoulder like we were designed to fit together. "So. Yeah, my excellence aside, I went to dig them up and see if I could remember which gift was which, and ..."

"Your gifts for your sisters."

"My gifts for my sisters," they agreed. "It's your fault, honestly. All this peaceful paddling over the waves and calm vibes, not to mention the generous, loving family shit. I thought, well, hey, I'm out of Evelyn's hair like she wanted. Not there flaunting my ... whatever, the opposite of being a conservative, proper Texan lady shit is in her face. So I called her to see if I could just take Cass and Stell to lunch one day, give them their presents. I'd rent a car if she agreed."

"I don't care about the car. I mean, you can take it anytime. Or I'll drive you."

"Thanks, but it's pointless. She won't let me anywhere near them. Said if I mail the gifts, she'll be sure they get them."

I was practically out the door, ready to drive to this horror show woman's house and climb the roof in a Santa suit to drop those obviously curated, special gifts down the chimney and directly into Andi's sisters' hands.

Instead, I took a solid breath. "So. What do you want to do?"

FOURTEEN

What did I want to do?

Carefully pack back up the gifts. And while I was at it, carefully pack up the visual, and tactile, and olfactory sensations of a bare-chested Cole. Just in case I wanted to examine those sensations again at a later date. In private. Or in a neat little duo of me and Cole, because suddenly, somehow, I could think up a lot of intriguing scenarios involving the two of us.

Me and Cole. Who knew?

I pulled away from his warmth. "Didn't my agenda say it's cookie decorating this afternoon?"

His smile bloomed, like he'd never in his thirty-odd years heard something more delightful. Which I knew wasn't the case, now after his affirming experience with his baby nephew. That qualified as a truly delightful moment, not my running away from my family problems by immersing myself in his family's wholesomeness.

"Okay, hold on to that competitive spirit. Margo is a genius with the piping bag, and the rest of us scramble to take second place."

I rubbed my hands together like I'd ever made a home-made cookie in my life. "Bring it on."

I holed up at the kitchen counter working for a couple of hours before we walked over, Cole promising we could get a lift back after dinner, "or anytime you want to leave," but it wasn't like it was far. I routinely walked further from my Fishtown apartment to the MFL to commute to work, and that was in Philly weather. So Cole didn't need to hover protectively and lay out six hundred scenarios for my comfort and escape.

And if he thought he'd hidden his impulses to go yell at my stepmother, he was wrong-headed about that, too.

I didn't need his solicitude, and I didn't need his valor. I did need the distraction of detailed descriptions of various baked goods, which is what I got once we'd made it past the gauntlet of greetings and into the Dunway family kitchen. Margo made a face at her brother and took me under her wing. Put me under her command, in truth, but in a low-key and genial way that felt way more acceptable than how Cole thought he should be the one in charge of everything. His sister knew how to invite my cooperation in her schemes.

She did not know how to teach me her wizard ways with the decorative icing, but I got into a rhythm with adding the sprinkles and moving trays to and from her work area. It was ... congenial, working away with her and the others, feeling a part of things, while we mixed and baked and sang along to the Christmas carols playlist.

And I managed to be stunned into silence, and stillness, when Scorch Madigan came in, joining the song and nudging Margo to snatch the reindeer cookie she'd just finished adding a face to. Not that I'd forgotten about him.

Cole had mentioned his other sisters would arrive by dinnertime, so he was part of that expectation.

The disjointedness of a famous singer—singers, because Brendan Brody came in right behind Scorch, with two women who were so clearly the other Dunway sisters —appearing like any other casual guy getting a pre-dinner sugar fix was enough to shut my systems down. Long enough that Cole slid up next to me and took a tray of gingerbread Santas out of my hands. "You okay?"

More solicitude. I gave him a look to convey how much I didn't need that from him.

He grinned like I was hilarious. "Sarita, Ignatius, Jeannie, and Brendan, meet Andi. They're a friend from Philly."

Scorch—or Ignatius, since apparently we didn't use stage names while doing wholesome family holiday activities—wriggled his fingers in a wave while he scarfed the cookie. The others offered various greetings, and I nodded and social nicetied my way back to a semblance of participation in the discussion.

After all the chatter about how was the drive in and did they see how the neighbors up the road were trying to outdo Uncle Bill with their light display and so on, I was comfortably back behind my spot at the kitchen island, sliding sugar cookies from the cooling rack to the tray for Margo to decorate. Brendan had slipped on an apron and taken over mixing dough from Cole, who'd stopped the cookie making to get everyone drinks. He launched into an easy conversation about the first holidays he'd spent in Rockport, and how many times he'd caught sight of the overwintering Whooping Cranes dancing.

"He's making that up," Scorch said, elbowing Brendan aside. "If a Whooper takes two steps, he claims it's dancing."

"It's a distinctive dance, Ignatius. I sent you the video."

"Deep fake. Go on, show Andi. They'll tell you." And then, like it wasn't enough that Scorch Madigan wasn't misgendering me, he grabbed my elbow. "Andi. Listen. This is important."

I swallowed my nerve and decided, fine, I would just no longer be star struck. "Okay?"

"When we came in, you were holding a bunch of cookies."

Brendan snorted. "Bro, look around you. We're surrounded by cookies."

"By thumbprint cookies, and white chocolate cranberry ones, and peanut butter balls, and every sugar cookie in the world. But ..." He leaned in and lowered his voice. "What happened to the gingerbread Santas? I saw you had them. I can still smell them in the air, but are they here? I think not. And if I ask Sarita, she'll get all smug about that time I said I didn't like Christmas cookies."

"You mean that time you were out Humbugging Scrooge?" Brendan's laugh, like his singing voice, was full of delicious low bass notes.

Cole showed up in the kitchen just then and stopped short. His face softened, the line of his beard shifting like he was hiding a smile, and he leaned against the doorframe. "You good?"

"You keep asking me that." Annoyingly, my reply didn't sound at all annoyed.

He released the smile. "I'm a pest like that."

Ignatius shook my elbow a little. "Ignore him. He is a pest."

"Ah, but he's the one who took the goods. It turns out we need his intel."

As one, we turned to Cole, who pushed up his sleeves—gah, forearms—crossed his arms, and tipped his chin. "What do you need, and what's it worth to you?"

FIFTEEN

COLE

I came back from serving everyone clustered in the living room to find Margo raising a skeptical eyebrow at, I presumed, the way I kept hovering over Andi.

The problem with a sister you'd literally rode out a pandemic with was, she got too damn good at reading your every mood. And Margo seemed in no doubt about me being smitten. Worse, I didn't have much in the way of counterarguments to present.

Ignatius beckoned me close. "The gingerbread. Where is it?"

"Why are we whispering?"

"So your sister doesn't catch me. Obviously."

I turned to Andi. "Did he, or did he not, eat like four cookies while the rest of us were saying hi?"

"Leave them out of it. They're my ally here. If it weren't for Andi, I'd have no idea you were the one holding out on me."

It was something, seeing how relaxed Andi'd gotten about being in proximity to my famous brothers-in-law. They'd clearly had a moment when everyone first came in, but now, bracketed by the guys, they were not at all flustered. "Okay, I'll tell you. But first, y'all pose for a pic."

"What? Cole, no, that's ..."

Mostly ignoring Andi's blush, Ignatius, Brendan, and Margo scooted in to ham it up.

"Say 'Santa' on three."

I took several, so Andi could choose which they wanted to share with Jerome and the others. After pointing out the gingerbread, and leaving Margo and Brendan to do all the requisite teasing about how they'd been practically under Ignatius's nose, I gestured for Andi to follow me to the dining room.

"Are you extracting me for a reason?"

Damn if they didn't make me fizz with humor all the time. "Only to give you a breather. When everyone's home, it can get to be like there are Dunways and Dunway-adjacent people popping up in every corner. My uncle and his partner are showing up in a half-hour with dinner, so it'll be inescapable chaos."

Their nose wrinkled like I'd given them a huge conundrum. I didn't mind how they gazed off over my shoulder in thought, since it gave me more time to study the way the grey of their irises darkened to steel at the rims, and how their lashes swept in the exact same arc as their brows. But then they refocused on me and said, "I'll stay for dinner."

Like it was a gift they were giving to me, personally.

And I took it that way.

"Great. I'm glad. Thank you."

"Thanks for having me." Andi took a step towards me. I resisted closing the distance even more. "Your family is nice. And obviously, you figured out that I needed a distraction after talking to Evelyn."

"I would have, too. She seems like a piece of work."

"That's a polite way to put it. But she also controls my access to Cassiopeia and Estella, so."

I grimaced. "So."

"Exactly." Andi looked around the dining room. "But that's not a problem for today. Tell me how you're going to fit all eighty-six of you in here?"

I swept my arms wide. "Ah, you've discovered the one problem of being from a family that keeps on growing. It was tight enough for the eight of us when I was growing up—never mind if any of the relatives stopped by. Now we're fourteen, I think? No, wait, fifteen, with you and the baby. Seventeen when the uncles get here."

"Larissa's not coming," Emmeline said from behind me.

I whirled, which, since my arms were still gesturing to the tight confines of the dining room, meant I ended up with my arm around Andi's shoulders. "No?"

"Nope. Spencer had immunizations today, so they're taking it easy at home."

"Aw, my poor bud. I wanted to introduce Andi to him. And Alfie, of course."

Andi's hand rubbed my shoulder blade, which was sweet, and also was a bolt of fiery energy because of how casually and naturally they'd fitted themself against me. "We'll catch them next time."

Emmeline was brows up. I ignored her. She smirked like the baby sister she was. "Yeah, you two sure will."

Also like the baby sister she was, Emmers ignored my narrowed eyes. I shook my head. "So. Thirteen for dinner, which I'm pretty sure was a Poirot film, but I'll guarantee none of us are killers. And only about half of us will eat in here. We've got card tables Emmeline is probably supposed to be setting up in the living room now, instead of pestering us."

"I didn't think you'd grump out about me asking for help."

"A breather. All I wanted was a simple breather."

Andi nudged into me. "You said the breather was for me."

"I lied. Sarita and Jeannie kept asking me if I was really sure I like my job and is there anything they can do to make my life easier and what about a good winter coat because they know it gets cold and I probably was shivering ever since I moved there even though the family outfitted me with a ridiculous amount of down and thermal layers last Christmas."

We followed Emmeline into the living room while I griped. It was extra of me, but that's what happened whenever I spent a significant amount of time with a crowd of my sisters. They turned me into the puppy version of myself, always a little wriggly and excitable and snappish. Not that knowing they had that effect ever stopped me from falling into it.

"Cole, stop." That was Sarita, who held up her hand like the orchestra conductor she was, as she gestured with the other for Jeannie to cross in front of me and Andi with a couple of folding chairs. But then, instead of waving us forward, she grinned and pointed up.

At the mistletoe directly over our heads.

SIXTEEN

ANDI

ole's sister—strike that, a whole bevy of Cole's sisters—smirked at us.

So, that was a family trait, then.

He'd gone revealingly still under my hand. And the fact I was still anchored to Cole was revealing, too. It wasn't something I was racing to contemplate. Instead, I turned to face him, and caught the slight widening of his eyes when I braced myself on his biceps. By the time I'd leaned in, he'd caught up to my intentions.

It wasn't like it was a big deal. Sure, the family was bound to tease him about it, but they seemed bound to tease him, regardless. And a mistletoe kiss meant nothing special. It was only a holiday tradition, probably to do with some pagan rite or something feudal.

And, of course, he tasted both sweet and a little tangy. He'd been eating cookies and drinking beer. Plus, we were in a humid coastal city, so it made sense for his lips to be smooth and a little giving under mine. All those hours kayaking and whatever else he did to keep fit explained the flex of his muscles as I stroked up his shoulders.

Every logical defense fled, though, when I tried to rationalize away my breath-caught moan. And his little answering growl, soft enough for my ears only.

"Okay, move on, it's our turn," Brendan said, pulling Jeannie behind him as he closed in on us. He shot us a wink before wrapping his wife in a hug. I nodded in thanks, then retreated to where Emmeline was lifting a folding table. Cole followed, positioning the second table himself while his sister and I set up the first one.

That was the next couple of hours: being nearby each other, but not touching. Not talking about it. Listening to the family stories about people I'd meet at their party. Ignoring how contrived they were about me sitting next to Cole at dinner.

And then we walked back to the cottage, having managed almost no eye contact since the kiss, and not much conversation.

On the porch, Cole nudged his shoulder into mine. "Want to sit and listen to the waves for a while?"

The man was going to kill me with romance. And I'd dropped all my defense mechanisms so I could grab hold of him under the mistletoe. I nudged him right back and sat on the two-person bench. He didn't even glance at any of the single chairs he could have taken when he sat beside me.

"I'm back and forth, here, Andi. My family ... they think they know best. Which makes me a little aggravated. I want to growl and snap at them some, but ..." He sighed. "I really wanted to kiss you. So getting aggravated at their manipulation doesn't seem entirely fair on my part."

I let the gentle breeze play around us as I listened for the shush of waves.

Cole cleared his throat. "Now I've got this annoying

urge to be grateful to them, even though they're irritating AF. Worse, though, is that whatever is going on with me and them, it doesn't matter nearly as much to me as if there's something going on between us."

I hummed a noncommittal response, because I was enjoying all this confessional yearning of his. Unfair? Maybe, but I honored my own pleasures.

He leaned forward and braced his elbows on his knees. Focused on his clasped hands like they could stop him from sneaking more glances at me. "So, my first question is, are you still comfortable sharing the cottage with me? Because I can grab my stuff and head home."

"I thought there weren't any bedrooms left?"

One shoulder lifted in a shrug. "It's a sofa there, or a sofa here. Either way, shouldn't make a difference."

"Shouldn't?" What a telling word.

My question earned me one of those knowing Cole smiles. I gave up on soaking up the yearning vibes off him and pulled that move that always seemed sexy to me, of turning and swinging a leg up over his, so I straddled his lap. My knee hit the armrest, and I sucked in my breath, but Cole caught me around my hips, anchoring me.

"Oh, hon. Are you hurt?"

Instead of answering, I kissed him. It wasn't the soft, mostly polite meeting of lips from before dinner. His energy met mine, both of us surging towards each other. Open mouths, tongues, a too-brief moment of him catching my lower lip between his teeth and nipping down.

Within seconds, my knee didn't hurt at all. My nerves were too busy buzzing with the feel of his lips on mine, his hands alternating between grasping my waist and running up my spine, his thighs pressed tight between mine.

His kisses turned light and focused, tracing across my

cheek and down the fluttering pulse of my neck. I gasped and dropped my head to the side, granting him more access. His finger edged under my shirt to stroke the bare skin at the small of my back, which was so deliciously shivery that I couldn't hold in my moan. And didn't want to stop myself from grinding my lap down into his.

"Andi, hell."

"I'm not aggravated at your sisters. For the record."

Cole's laugh drowned out the breeze, the waves, the thudding of my heart. "I'm glad to know it."

"And if you like, you don't need to sleep on any of the available sofas."

At that, he went still and his hand tightened on my thigh as if he was driven to hold on to me. His eyes searched mine in the low light. "I don't?"

"If you like."

His chest expanded, and he pressed one gentle kiss to my cheek. "I like."

CHAPTER

SEVENTEEN

COLE

I was in some kind of holiday magic zone and it made me a little shaky about us leaving the porch. Which was appallingly sappy ammo I would never give my sisters, but my goals instantly shifted to ones that had nothing to do with my family.

Andi's tender look was morphing into a bit of a challenging smirk, and I couldn't have that. Not if I could have them, which apparently, I could. So I held them close and shifted to the edge of the chair.

They yelped. "Hey. Stop, what are you doing?"

Much as I'd have loved some showing off by standing with them in my arms, I knew my limits. "Teasing. Because you've made me happy, and apparently I tease when I'm happy." I helped them to their feet, crowded them as we toed our shoes off, and followed close as we went into the cottage.

"You're ridiculous."

"Probably. If that's a turn-off, I can try to rein it in."

Their eyes sparkled as they shot a look over their shoulder. "I'll let you know."

Yeah, it was absolutely magic. I caught Andi's hand. "If you change your mind at any point, I'll move back to the sofa. Or over to the house. It's in your control."

They stroked their free hand up to my nape. "Your control, too. I'm not assuming that you following me to my bed means you're up for anything in particular."

Damn, they were so tender and kind, and it was currently so unnecessary. "I think you'll find that I am up for anything in particular. But thank you."

And that was the end of polite restraint from us both. We smacked into the wall, stumbling while kissing our way to the bedroom. It wasn't a big enough cottage for us to get so turned around navigating, but our eyes and hands and bodies weren't free to pay attention to things like the logistics of where in space anything was. But since it wasn't a big cottage, we managed to land on the bed, curled together as my blood flared with each one of Andi's touches.

They gave fantastic touches.

I wrestled off my shirt, not at all calm about it, but it was more important to make more of myself available for those touches than it was to embody some semblance of urbane smoothness or whatever.

Their hands went to my shoulders and brushed down to my pecs. "Okay?"

"That's my line."

They smirked then. "Yeah, you stay in my business. I've been meaning to have that conversation."

Probably they were kidding. I kissed their palm and set it back over my heart. "At the risk of you reprimanding me again, can I ask about intimacy? What you're into?"

"And what you're into, I hope."

"I know what I'm into. I'm looking at what I'm into."

"Smooth." Their tone was dry as the needles on an unwatered Christmas tree. But they also hooked a thigh over my leg and kept that compelling rhythm of strokes from my chest up to my neck and back down again.

"Yes. People often remark about what a suave lover I am. Didn't Jerome pass that note on along with the rest of my file?"

"You're the one who compiles dossiers. The rest of us just gossip."

"About my seductive prowess. I know."

Andi tweaked my nipple at that, which was as good an opening as I was going to get. I traced the faint white lines of one of my surgical scars. "Okay, so—here I go, assuming you're a little familiar with top surgery?"

They nodded. "You're not the first trans person I've been to bed with, Cole."

"And there I was feeling all special. Was it ...? No, don't tell me, none of my business. Anyway, I know a lot of guys who had double incision, and maybe lose some sensation, at least at first. But mine was keyhole, and, yeah, my nipples? Sensitive AF. Maybe more than they even were before the surgery, but that might be lingering dysphoria coloring my memories. Point is, if you're going to tweak my nipple, be prepared for me to writhe a bit. In a good way. Unless your hands are cold, in which case, fuck right off cause I have a hell of a time when they get cold."

Andi flopped to the pillow, hands over their eyes.

"Are you laughing? This is me being vulnerable and honest and letting you in on the intimacies of my body, and you're laughing?"

"Telling me I can fuck right off is your version of vulnerability? Wow."

"Shush."

"So tender, so open. I am humbled to be taken into your confidences, Cole."

I straddled them and held a throw pillow up threateningly. "I'll show you humble."

They tweaked my nipples. Both of them. And they weren't gentle. I nearly jumped off them. "Gah!"

"You promised me writhing. That was more like when the vacuum scares my cat."

I abandoned the throw pillow. "You have a cat. How come I didn't know you have a cat?"

"Moscato. He's slinky and sneaky and my roommate resents him. But she's taking care of him this week, anyway. Or letting her cousin, who's staying in my room, do it."

They had a cat named Moscato. I had to pin them with my body weight and kiss their appallingly cute face. And then I had to kiss down their neck, where the scents of baking and sugar lingered, and stroke their arms, to encourage the way they explored my back.

As I discovered ways to make Andi squirm—my tongue on the pulse point of their neck, my fingers running light traces on the skin just under their ribs—their body relaxed under mine. We were shifting and touching and kissing and, yes, writhing.

And I wanted so much more.

CHAPTER

EIGHTEEN

ANDI

I broke away from Cole's mouth with a reluctant gasp. "Why are you groaning like there's something bad happening?"

His eyes were blown wide and darker than ever, and I anchored my hands to his ass—it gave me something firm and sexy to hold on to while I figured out if this was happening. Also, because if it wasn't happening, I at least deserved the memory of holding his ass as he pressed his crotch into mine like he had no choice but to grind into me.

"I do not classify anything happening here as bad."

My fingers flexed, which only made his hips thrust harder. I had to smile. "So far, I agree."

"You're killing me." He dropped his forehead to mine. "And I'm glad. Did I mention that I'm glad?"

"You talk a lot. I mean, I knew you talked a lot, but I thought once I got you into bed, you might … talk less?"

"And do more, you mean?" Even with his eyes closed, I caught the glinting intent behind his words.

"Well, here I am, fully clothed, and I've only gotten you out of your shirt."

With that, Cole sat up and set about unbuttoning me. "The inequity of it all. Let's fix things."

I shrugged a shoulder at a time, to help him draw my sleeves down, and a little, too, because I wanted to hide the full body shivers that raced up me as his deft fingers exposed more and more of my skin.

"The thing is," he said, pausing at my cuff to meet my gaze again. "I didn't come home for the holidays expecting I'd end up having sex with anyone."

I swallowed against the way his voice had gone all gravel and heat. It wasn't a surprise that Cole's highhandedness assurance that he knew what was best in every situation carried through to when he was in bed. I just hadn't expected that it would make me all gooey, when in every non-fucking scenario, I found it eye-rolling at best. "No?"

"No. So I didn't pack for this. I didn't even pack anything for solo play with my junk. Which is what I call my dick and my hole, by the way." He went back to unfastening the last of my buttons. I let him strip off my sleeves and wrapped my arms over his shoulders. "And you won't tell me what you like."

His words were one thing. The way his hands and lips and gaze took me in and spun my desire higher and higher was another thing entirely.

I wanted Cole Dunway. And here he was, hovering above me. Generous with his body, but not taking all the liberties I'd granted him with mine.

"So far, I like everything. It's not that I don't appreciate the questions."

"Is it the pace? Am I rushing you?"

"There you go, asking thoughtful questions about pleasure and consent while groping me."

He groaned again, rolling to lie at my side. "Andi. Help me out here."

I hooked a finger through his belt loop. "Can I help it if you're fun to harass? I got the impression from your family that you're used to it."

"Do not bring my sisters into this conversation, I beg of you."

I flat-out giggled. He kissed me and I gasped instead. "Fine, sibling talk is off-limits. And I appreciate the information about your terms and your sensitive nipples. Mine are sensitive, too, by the way. Which you'd have discovered by now if you hadn't stopped undressing me at just my shirt."

He closed his eyes like it could shield him from my teasing. "Andi …"

"But." I drew a little circle around his navel and unbuttoned his jeans. "You're asking, I bet, if I've got things I don't like in bed. I do, but since you apparently didn't pack your strap-on, it doesn't much matter that I don't like penetration."

"Mainly I meant lube, but that's good to know."

"So you do have a strap-on."

His grin was a thing of beauty. "Hon. My toy collection is varied and vast. If there's even a chance it can bring me or my partner's pleasure, I've got it."

I wriggled closer and worked my hand between his waistband and his boxers. The man's ass was as compelling as his statement. "Also good to know."

"I like pleasure. Giving it, receiving it." He raised his eyebrows. "Giving it again."

"You talk a big game for someone who could be on his way to his second orgasm by now. Here's my facts, Cole. I had a full sexual check up after a fun summer. All's good, no risks since then. You already found out how sensitive my neck is. My breasts are, too. My clit, even more so—and you can call them my breasts and clit, but nothing much more gendered than that. Touching the back of my knees doesn't do much for me, and neither does anything to do with my holes. My feet are ticklish. And I want to have sex with you. I want that pleasure you keep promising. If you have more preferences, please share them. If you'd like to tell me more secrets about your body, I'd love to hear it. If you want me to discover it as we explore each other, I'm up for that, too." I searched his face. "Is that enough info for you?"

In answer—I hoped it was in answer, because edging wasn't my thing and he was drawing all this out forever—Cole unzipped and shucked his jeans, leaving him in boxers and socks and a welcome, wicked smile.

As soon as I'd stripped off my sports bra and my own jeans, we were very close to fulfilling the fantasy that'd struck me when he'd strolled out of the shower all hot and damp and barely clad.

NINETEEN

COLE

Damn. Andi's idea about discovery via action instead of words: genius. I stopped wasting time and started kissing my way from their neck to their breasts. In return, they went straight back to my butt, and I made a mental note about never skipping squats again.

I sucked in my breath when I laved their nipples, and Andi cried out. "You didn't lie about your own responsiveness."

Their grip had moved, as I lowered myself along their torso, to my shoulder and my hair. Now they shook my head a bit. "You said you were going to give me pleasure. It would please me if you'd stop bantering and get on with it."

They made me laugh so fucking much. I licked my lips and dove back in. The super sweet sugar cookie scent faded until all I inhaled was Andi's usual honeyed warmth. It went to my head, or having their whole length bared to me did. It was more, though, than just the fun of intimacy. As much as I liked sex, I rarely went into it with my heart thrashing quite so much.

But the moment Andi's lips met mine under the mistletoe, I started vibrating on a new frequency. Something tender mixed in with the horniness; something intense deepening the pleasure of mutual attraction.

And now their hands stroked their approval as I meandered across their belly and nuzzled to their core. Their legs wrapped round mine in welcome as I feathered kisses at the crease of their thighs. Their consent flew my way as I hummed a question about stripping them out of their underwear.

And then their thighs clamped to my head, stopping me in my lust-fueled tracks. "Um, Andi?"

They tugged my hair. "Beard. Tickles."

I turned my head just enough to slide my cheek along their inner thigh. "Oh?"

"Cole." There was something urgent in their voice, which, combined with the way their pelvis was a softening assault to my senses, spurred me to more mischief.

I scraped my other cheek across their other thigh. Darted out my tongue, licking lightly at the skin I'd just abraded. Andi's legs fell open again, and I took it as the freedom I craved to explore their most intimate places. Thighs, hips, glistening curls. With my fingers, my mouth. My beard. Nuzzling, I let my nose lead the way to their clit, which responded to my breath with more wetness between their folds.

"Can I taste you here, Andi? Would you like if my tongue circled you, and if my fingers traced the radiating arms of your clit? Will you tell me what you like, or do I have to—do I get to—experiment to figure it out?"

"Talking. Always so much talking."

I had to talk, because my smile was too wide for me to follow through on any of my promised explorations. I surged up to kiss their mouth, to show them how turned on I was, and how delighted that I got to explore their reactions. I was fucking giddy.

And by the time I worked my way back down Andi's body, their hips were pulsing in a rhythm it thrilled me to mimic as I finally—finally—applied my mouth to the pearl of their glans. They jerked in a throughly satisfying way when I tapped them with the flat of my tongue, so I resolved to always use that move.

I'd already resolved to have much more sex with Andi Ennis. It was my primary goal to convince them I was a good bet.

So I tapped, and I touched, and I listened and tasted and felt. I tracked each of Andi's reactions, cataloging and heightening and savoring every one.

Their moans got less verbal, their breaths faster and more broken. I toyed with their nipple while sneaking a look up their torso, memorizing the shifts of their body when they strained towards climax.

When Andi came, my heart was swooping and soaring within my chest. I petted their clit sweetly as they came down, dropped kisses on their curls and their navel and that precious spot between their breasts. I lingered there, entranced by their long exhale and the fluttering pulse at their neck.

At last I fell to the pillow beside them. Andi scraped fingers through my hair, then placed their fingers against my lips.

I raised my eyebrows.

"You're about to ask me if I'm okay. You have a compulsion about asking me that."

I rolled in my lips, which they could tell just fine with their hand still covering my mouth.

"I knew it. Cole Dunway: gives stellar head, refuses to take all the nonverbal cues that he did well."

"Hey." I propped up on my elbow. "I already acknowledged my sexual prowess. My question was going to be about your emotional state, not your physical one."

They rolled their eyes, like I needed an emoji-level demonstration of their opinion, when I'd thought I was being considerate. "Cole. You're not my therapist. And I haven't had to talk to her about my feelings about sex in a good few years. Can you try to trust that once we decided to go to bed together, I was all-in on the whole of this situation?"

Slayed, and put in my place. Andi's deft mind was fast becoming one of my favorite things about them. I leaned down for another kiss, ready to take their lead on all that came next.

CHAPTER
TWENTY

ANDI

Somewhere along the way, I'd lost my bones. Lost my muscles, too, maybe.

But not my nerves. No, they were all alive and on alert and extremely, extraordinarily pleased by all that Cole had done to me.

I lingered over our kiss, willing myself to re-energize. There was so much more I wanted to experience with him.

Starting with the slight rasp of his beard as I explored the clean edge between it and his cheek. The tickling scrape under my bottom lip, against the mobile smoothness of my top lip. I hovered over Cole, catching his earlobe between my teeth, squeezing his ribs between my knees.

"Andi, fuck." He'd loosened my topknot, and was running his hands through my hair. Letting it fall to cover our faces, then pulling it away, over and over again. Hide, find, hide again. If I'd had a bit of focus to spare beyond what was happening in the tight space we shared, I could try to sort out why such a simple action was winding me up.

But I didn't, so I enjoyed the ride. Made it rockier by

giving his nipples the attention he seemed to crave. The promised writhing? Everything I'd hoped for. Cole loved being held down and teased, and it turned out I loved doing it to him. Bossy as he was, he'd never have come out and said it, and I wondered if, for all his ease with his libido and the chemistry between us, he even knew how much he'd like me getting all toppy with him.

I captured his nipples between thumbs and forefingers and stopped moving. "Time for you to answer some of my questions."

"Yes, I consent, get on with it." His voice had dropped to that gravel range, but he still whined.

"Patience."

"Fuck."

"That's the plan. Now. Tell me. If you'd packed more wisely, would I be strapped into a dildo and fucking your hole right now?"

His torso tried to spasm, but I held him tight. "I ... if that was what you wanted."

When I loosed my fingers, he shook his head rapidly, then nodded once. "Yes."

"You didn't pack well, though, did you?"

His sigh was epic. "If only."

I kissed him and reasserted my pinch hold. "So now I only get to play with my fingers and mouth, since you also don't have lube?"

"You don't either," he pointed out. Then lifted his brows. "Or do you?"

I laughed. "Alas, no. We are bereft."

I slid my legs apart and shifted so our crotches met. He was still wearing his boxers—and one sock, which left me inordinately tender towards him.

"I wouldn't have said bereft is the predominant feeling I'm experiencing right now."

Trailing my hands down his chest and tucking my fingers under his waistband, I cocked my head at him. "No?"

Slowly—deliberately—Cole licked his lips and bit down on the lower one. He shook his head.

"What are you feeling, then?"

"Andi." It was more of a demand than a whine this time. I had to press my mouth tight to contain my laugh.

"Thought you were the talkative one in this bed. Here I am, inviting you to detail all the ways you need me to take care of you, and all you can say is my name?"

"When I die from unfulfilled lust, you're the one who'll have to explain things. Good luck asking Jerome and Sybil to let you live it down."

Ridiculous, petulant, beautiful man. Fast as I could manage, I yanked down his boxers and pressed the heel of my hand against his dick. Cole threw his head back, bucking his hips and groaning.

"You want me to get you off, Cole? You want me to explore and guess and follow my own whims without any of your smart-ass labels and instructions?" I wasn't asking to hear his answer. I was asking so his breath would keep stuttering and his fists would stay clenched at his sides like he'd forgotten how to use all his hard-won muscles to do anything about his own need.

I kissed my way down his torso, detouring so very briefly to suck on each nipple, while keeping a rocking pressure on his core. It wasn't until I'd straddled his leg so I could rut against it, that I let go and laced my fingers through his.

When I kissed his hip, he hissed. "Andi."

"You keep saying that." I kissed his other hip. Blew on his engorged sex. His hands lifted in mine, not going anywhere, but clearly in search of a place to land. I guided them to his chest. "Make yourself useful."

And then I grabbed his ass and sucked him into my mouth.

It turned out that exploring and guessing was more than good enough for him. It wasn't much work to discover that Cole liked pressure, and he loved being sucked off, and he was pretty keen on playing with himself while all that happened. I had him coming with a few determined strokes, and nearly set myself off again in the process. Once Cole took on the role of the boneless one in the bed, I curled into his side and gave myself a lazy orgasm. And then neither of us had bones again, only gentle lips, and quiet, contented hums, and the slow tracing of fingers on cooling skin.

Packing woes aside, it was turning out to be not at all the holiday trip I'd feared.

CHAPTER
TWENTY-ONE
COLE

We woke slowly, long after the winter sun warmed the windows. I had my arms around Andi, and my nose buried in their hair.

I liked it way much.

They huffed out a breath when I kissed their shoulder, but they'd been playing with the hair on my arms, so I knew I wasn't waking them. When I leaned up to nuzzle at their temple, they stretched and slanted a smile my way.

"Are you looking for round three before we've even brushed our teeth?"

"I really, really wish I was. It's the tamalada today. I've got to get up to the house. Do you want to come?"

They shook their head. "I do, but I've gonna do some work."

"If that's code for, 'I'm going to persuade you to stay in bed with me all day,' I've got some work to do, too."

They moved my questing hands away. "No, but nice try. I'm not getting us into trouble for you being late. I heard your parents talking about all the logistics last night."

I groaned, because they were far too right. Not that

anyone needed my tamal-rolling prowess. Our family was full of people who were sure they knew more about the art than anyone else. But after that display of ours under the mistletoe, my sisters would line up, waiting for the chisme. I wasn't subjecting Andi to the worst of their nonsense, so it was better if I placated their need for gossip on my own.

Emmeline opened the door as I came up the walk. "You're swaggering. It's gross, stop it."

I stopped. "Swaggering?"

She nodded. "You're too self satisfied for nine in the morning. You're walking like your limbs are all loose. We don't need a play-by-play of our brother's sex life."

I wrapped her in a hug she pretended to fend off. "I would never subject you to such a thing. Unlike some of our sibs, I know how to be discreet."

She shoved me through the doorway. "I'm the only discreet one in this family, but you're welcome to join me on the side of the angels."

That gave me pause. "Emmers? Do you have something to share with the sibs?"

Larissa caught my question and threw her arms up in a giant X. "No. My baby sister is pure as the driven snow. Her interests are only intellectual, and she's never been tempted by anything ... earthy."

Emmeline snorted. "Whatever you say."

I followed them to the kitchen to grab coffee and a couple of the breakfast burritos that Larissa and Alfie Senior always brought to the tamalada. I'd tried to use them to lure Andi, but they'd insisted they were fine scrounging breakfast from whatever was in the cottage.

Margo was at the kitchen island, chopping tomatoes for salsa, while Karl and Brendan washed dishes and Jeannie soaked more corn husks.

I popped through to the dining room. "Morning, everyone."

Mama, Aunt Max, Uncle Bill, Alfie Senior, Ignatius, and Emmeline sat around the table, which groaned under the weight of bowls of masa and filling ingredients. Four instant pots lined the sideboard, two of them already at work steaming the first batches of tamales. I made the rounds to kiss everybody and find out who needed refills or supplies or a break from the production line.

Alfie wanted to check on the kids, so I slipped into his spot and took over, adding the filling atop the strip of masa that Ignatius had spread on the corn husks. Then I slid them along to Uncle Bill so he could roll them into neat packages that he arranged in a steamer basket.

Across from our chicken verde production line, the others filled tamales with Aunt Max's pulled pork recipe. I held one of my breakfast tacos across to Aunt Max so she could spoon a dollop of her filling atop my eggs. It meant a scolding, but it also meant I got to make heart eyes at Maxima, so she knew my undying devotion to her filling.

It was a bare minute of general banter later before Margo and Sarita maneuvered themselves into the seats flanking me. I was choosing to ignore their expectant glances until the third time Margo bopped me on the arm in the process of sliding over a prepped corn husk. I gave up. "You're impossible, you know that?"

"I mean, I'm extraordinary, but impossible?"

"Hilarious."

"I am unique, extraordinary, and hilarious," she agreed. "Now tell us what happened with you and Andi."

"I can't. Emmers told me it would be gross."

Serita's laugh drew too many elder eyes, so Gogo and I hissed her to silence.

Emmeline leaned across. "All I told him was if he can't convey facts without bragging, he's not worthy of them."

"I wasn't actually asking for my personal life to become y'alls business, you know. You're the ones who connived to make our first kiss so public."

"Connived?" Margo said, eyebrows raised. "Wow."

"First kiss?" Sarita's tone was all innocence. "How many kisses, exactly, were there?"

I narrowed my eyes at her. "It would be ungentlemanly of me to answer that, and y'all know I am a perfect gentleman."

None of my sisters tried to contain their laughter at that, which meant open season on the general discourse about my love life. By the time our row had switched over to filling sweet pumpkin tamales, I'd admitted to more than a few kisses.

And, I hoped, persuaded them all that treating Andi any differently because of it was a sure way of making them feel unwelcome, when they had already been dealing with the problem of being unwelcome by a family for the holidays.

TWENTY-TWO

ANDI

I was having feelings, and I didn't like it.

Not about Cole, but about all his familial holiday traditions. Dad and I'd had traditions. Sort of. They were ones that didn't involve elaborate setups, or days of advanced preparation, or crowds of revelers. Putting hot cocoa in thermoses and driving around the fancily lit neighborhoods. Our blanket fort movie time. Assembling snowflake decorations from paper and popsicle sticks and too much glitter.

He showered me with material goods, too—took me skiing over a few winter breaks, kept me in top-notch electronics—but that wasn't what stuck with me. Instead, it was the way we kept one of the hall closets stuffed with every old comforter and sleeping bag and lap throw we never needed in Houston's temperate climate, all so that once a year, we could pull them all out to make the sploogiest, most epically misshapen fort ever.

When Evelyn moved in, cleaning out that closet had been part of her process to put her own mark on the house. I'd already heard, "Andromeda, don't make such a fuss," from her about a dozen other things, so when she emptied the entire linen closet and started shoving most of it towards the trash and donate piles, I retreated to my room. It wasn't until we were bringing the holiday decorations out of the attic that next December that I saw Dad had filled three oversize bins with our blanket fort supplies.

Evelyn even contributed some of her seasonal throw pillows and a quilt from some relative of hers that had been lurking in the newly tidy linen closet to our construction. And once my sisters came along, she sat in the fort with us long enough to watch at least half the movie. So, it wasn't cookie making, or party prep, or an elaborately decorated tree, but we'd had our traditions. And I'd thought, since Evelyn was doing Christmas at home with the girls for the first time since Dad died, that I'd be helping them carry them on.

Instead, I was three hours south of my sisters, while Cole's entirely nice and festive family had their fun, and I didn't know if my sisters even remembered how Dad made the same joke about The Grinch stealing his stockings every time he pulled on some of his mis-matched holiday themed socks.

I didn't check off—didn't want to check off—many of the boxes of the mainstream traditional American, but: I missed my dad. I missed my sisters. I was fucking furious that Evelyn had smashed in my hope of spending some time strengthening the holiday memories that he had made with us.

So in between dealing with work emails, I poured all that out on my fic, as much as I could. Because on top of feeling all too barreled over by sentiment, I was having feelings about Cole.

They were warm and gooey feelings, like those ridiculously tasty walnut chocolate chunk cookies we'd made. And I didn't want my family of origin feelings spiking through anything that was going on with the feelings I was finding with him.

He lured me back to his family's house with photos of tamales and the promise of "the best margaritas you've ever had." Following the music through the open door, I found much of what was turning out to be the usual crowd, this time including a couple of little kids. So that made the one in the ponytail, nursing on the sofa, the oldest sister. Larissa. She waggled her fingers over the baby's head in greeting, and I sat beside her to introduce myself. And get a gander at the baby that looked like Cole.

Joke was on me, since she seemed to have my entire biography at her fingertips. Apparently, Cole's dossiers went both ways.

He emerged then, from the kitchen or backyard or wherever else. "Andi."

Larissa's smirk proved I wasn't the only one noticing the pleasure in his voice.

"You promised me margaritas."

"By all means," he said, almost bowing at me. Fool. I got up and followed him to the kitchen. It was unoccupied, which seemed like a little holiday miracle from all I knew about the Dunways so far. So we seized the chance and stole a few kisses before Cole got me my drink. He also dropped a plate of tamales and rice on the island in front of me.

"Aren't we having dinner in like an hour?"

"Yeah, but the rest of us have been snacking all day. Dinner's basically three carrots each. You need to catch up or you'll get the midnight munchies."

I swallowed my urge to tease him about our mouths

and midnight, since no room in the house stayed empty for long. The way he bit his lips suggested he had his own ideas about what we'd get up to later that night.

The sisters married to rock stars showed in the kitchen then, going straight for the blender of frozen margaritas. Their husbands were on their heels, and from the looks on everyone's faces, I braced for … something. Cole had promised, as if the behavior of his entire family was absolutely under his control in a way that could never lead to his heart being shattered by broken expectations, that no one would tease us about getting together.

That didn't mean they wouldn't pry into my feelings. Or do some weird 'if you hurt my brother, I'll avenge him' nonsense. Or just stare avidly between us like we were a Wimbledon final, looking for the faults that would break us.

I'd braced for one or all of those options when Ignatius parked himself between us, shoulder to shoulder to shoulder, and drummed so emphatically on the counter my drink sloshed over the salt-encrusted rim of the cup.

"Andi? Andi, Andi, Andi." He looked at Cole, passed me a napkin, nudged me. "Andi Cole's friend from Philly. I have such an important question for you."

I tried—and failed—to parse anyone's mood. "Okay?"

"Are you LuminousDust?"

CHAPTER

TWENTY-THREE

COLE

I didn't know what Ignatius was talking about, but Andi's face flamed and they shrank in a completely unacceptable way. I pushed him aside and took Andi's hands, which were too cold to blame on the frozen drink. "Need me to get you out of here? We can go through the back."

They resisted my tugs, though. On a vast exhale, they shook their head. "I'm fine. It's okay."

I bit back eighteen ways to rephrase the question, none of which proved I believed them, but was still determined to shield them from whatever in Ignatius's question had hit them like a stealth attack. Instead, I glared at my brother-in-law, who'd held up his hands like I was being unreasonable and silly, but he wasn't going to puff up about it.

Which meant I'd gone overboard. I settled down, but anchored myself to Andi's side. Ignatius would not get between us again.

"I think that answers our question," Brendan said. "And now I want to shake your hand."

He reached out like he wasn't being just as weird as

92

Ignatius. Andi relaxed, though, and took Brendan's outstretched hand.

"My turn." Ignatius took Andi's other hand. And somehow, they let my brothers-in-law tug them into the dining room. Never mind that I'd failed to lead Andi anywhere else myself. I gathered their plate and our drinks and followed.

"My manager sends me this stuff, bullet points of interest. Couple years back, one of them was a link to your fic." Brendan was going full animation, which was normally something he reserved for the stage. Or time with just him and Jeannie. "So I called Scorch up and read him some of it."

Andi buried their head in their hands.

I glared at them all, but took the phone Sarita handed me. The site tagged Scorch Madigan's fandom, but the story was ... "Is this set in space?"

Ignatius pointed at me. "Exactly, yes, onboard the *Perseus*. They've created this whole amazing AU where I'm Captain Kindle Cable-Kitching, and I pilot a rebel ship. We broke with the Marius Federation because I—or CKC-K, who's this awesome leader. So, she's got a way of seeing eighteen steps ahead to know how the Marius Federation is plotting evil, and she told the crew of *Perseus* about it, and they all agreed to go rogue with her, but then it took a while for others in the Federation to know it was justified. But now CKC-K is getting all these overtures from some of the same people who trashed her when the Marius Federation heads planted false stories about her. So now she and the crew have to figure out all the diplomacy and who they can trust."

I took it in as logically as I could, pairing it with Ignatius's career history. "So the Federation leaders are your old band?"

"Yeah, I mean, we always figured LuminousDust—Andi—started there, but they've expanded it into this entire universe that's way better than my actual life. We're all addicted. Where's Margo? She'll tell you. We do dramatic readings on the tour bus. We call the bus Perseus because of this fic."

Andi made an inarticulate noise and stared at him. "That's ... you do not."

"Ask Margo. Go on."

I pulled out my phone and texted her. A moment later, Gogo stepped into the dining room. "Why are you asking about Perseus?"

Brendan and Ignatius talked over each other. Sarita handed over her phone, and I scooted closer to Andi.

"I am being very restrained and not asking if you're okay."

That got a laugh out of them. "I'd say I was proud of you, but that would only encourage you to brag on yourself even more."

I played at haughtiness. "I never brag."

"Andi's the one who should brag," Sarita said. "We really love your writing."

"I should brag." Ignatius puffed out his chest. "I'm the one who figured out LuminousDust must be Andi."

They shook their head. "How, though?"

"Because CKC-K's never had a holiday cookie making party before. I loved the thing last year, with her and Science Officer Linden making that cozy celebration tent inside the off-duty lounge, but everyone trying to recreate home planet sweets to share? Including that hot bit where CKC-K says Linden's ginger cookies are her favorite? Plus, Andromeda Galaxy; Andi. It all fits."

"That's ... not that hard to figure out, I guess. If I'd

known you were reading, I wouldn't have written anything so obvious." They smirked a little, and it lit me up inside, seeing them relax into teasing with my family.

"Exactly. I'd have been the first to know, except Ignatius reads too fast. Plus, he had the fic open about two secs after we got the notification." Sarita shot her husband a look, because one thing we all learned by growing up in a house of six kids was how to be competitive. Ignatius just grinned in happy triumph.

"You all get notified? Wait, what are your pseuds? Have I been interacting with you all this time?" Andi closed their eyes tight. "Do not answer those questions. It's bad enough you all read it."

"Is it bad?" Jeannie, clearly jumping into big sister mode, gentled her voice. "I'm sorry if this all ambushed you. We don't want to make you self-conscious about it."

"You can't stop," Brendan said. "I need to know what's going to happen with Faure and Billy."

"Not helping," Jeannie said.

Andi passed him their phone. "Give me your number. I'll text it to you. I've got the next three chapters written. The cookie thing was just a spontaneous interlude."

The rest of them played grab and type, demanding Brendan not get any special treatment. It gave Andi, at last, a moment to eat their tamales.

Throughout the evening, with all my family's questions about Andi's writing, and the singing that started up after dinner, and walking home, hand-in-hand, under the stars, I did not one single time ask them if they were okay.

CHAPTER

TWENTY-FOUR

ANDI

We'd arranged to carpool into the shopping district, such as it was, so I got my slightly sex-buzzed body out of bed when the alarm went. Cole grumbled, but followed me to the shower, which was a sweet and sensual way to start the day.

It was getting to be too nice, how we kinda shared the same scents. The citrus of the shower gel, the nuttiness of the coffee. It'd been a long minute since I'd enmeshed my daily life with a partner's.

Not that we were partners. Not that we shared a daily life outside of these few out-of-time days. No matter what the group text was insinuating about the photos we'd shared. Once they got over exploding about Cole's famous relatives—or learned who they were, and then exploded, in the case of Jerome, who didn't follow music written after about 1880—it was a quick leap to the speculation. Which reminded me.

Andi: Turns out Scorch and Brendan Brody read LuminousDust

96

Liz: No! Way!

Jerome: ???

Cole: You told Liz?

Liz: [link to fic] It's a whole thing, J. You'll love it, but key point is, Andi writes a killer story and Cole's related to the inspiration behind it

Andi: Liz and I have shared fandoms

Sybil: Liz told me when A told them about LuminousDust

Jerome: of course she did

Jerome: and of course no one told me

Jerome: rude

Cole: no one told me

Andi: you don't strike me as a fandom guy. Anyway, quit texting and start driving, we're gonna be late

Cole pocketed his phone and got us underway. "We can't be late to a store. Stores are just there whenever."

I shrugged. "You promised to pick up your sisters three minutes ago."

"They won't be ready when we get there."

"Irrelevant." I stashed my phone, leaving a half-written draft so the group could get aggravated by the three bouncing dots for a bit. "And what matters is how now you're sitting there flinching a little every time your notifications buzz."

"Hilarious."

I didn't bother answering, since the others were piling into the car. Rockport had little in the way of a downtown. We gathered at what was apparently Larissa's favorite strips center and talked out a schedule for who would walk and who would drive to the other locations before we met for lunch.

Cole followed me into a stationery and gift shop, offering his expertise on his family and not taking any of my hints about leaving me alone so I could find something for him.

"You really don't need to buy anything," he said, because he was still selectively bad at listening to me.

"They've taken me in and fed me repeatedly. I'm buying your parents a gift. Don't you need to get anything?"

"No, I shipped it all home a couple of weeks ago. I just need more wrapping paper."

We reached a center with a jewelers and a bookstore. I spotted Emmeline emerging from the thrift shop at the end, carrying a box three times bigger than her head. "Looks like you're needed elsewhere. Will you put that in the trunk with her stuff?" I handed him my shopping bag, and he took off with his sister.

At last, a few sneaky minutes without him observing what I bought. He was maybe distracted, or he got the hint, because I bought his gift and stowed it in my backpack before we all reconvened at the diner.

It was as we were leaving lunch, full of chatter, that the Dunway sisters formed a flank around us, each more upright than the next. All of Cole's silly energy seemed to convert in a flash to bristling, and his hand tightened in mine.

The snide expression of the person facing us on the sidewalk hinted he was the problem. So did the way he slowly crossed his arms and looked Cole up and down, like he was seeing something distasteful.

"Well, howdy. Look at all the Dunways, riding together in a pack."

Yep. This person was the problem. I squeezed Cole's hand and leaned into him. "Buddy of yours?"

He snorted a little. "He's an ex."

The ex snorted right back. "You wish we'd had a relationship. This one followed me around for an entire summer."

"You coming by to pick him up every time you went to the beach or down to whatshername's house parties isn't what I'd call Cole following you around," Margo said.

"Neither was you sending him thirteen postcards during your eight-day trip to Charleston." Emmeline added, which made the rest of the sisters snicker.

Cole got even more rigid, and something clicked into place. I took a half-step forward. "Hey, nice to meet you. I'm Andi. They/them."

It wasn't what the ex had expected, and maybe more important, it wasn't what the Dunways expected. The phalanx of sisters loosened up, half of them retreating to Sarita's SUV. Cole's shoulders dropped just a tad.

"Right." The ex shook my hand. "Elliot. He/him."

I asked Elliot a couple of questions about Rockport. He deflected anything more than surface level, not that I actually cared about his answers. Cole threw in a comment about some mutual's move out of state. Six minutes later, we were back in the rental car.

"That guy was always a snotheaded irritant of the highest order," Emmeline declared. "You took the wind out of his sails, though."

Margo bumped her fist against my shoulder. "Truth. Nicely done."

I turned to regard them both. "Thanks. He wasn't my favorite new acquaintance in Rockport. But can I say one thing I noticed? Is that Cole didn't have much to say about him. And I'm wondering about that."

Margo was watching her brother, who'd put the ignition on but made no move to back us out of the parking lot. "About ... what?"

I focused on him, too. "Cole, sorry for delving. We don't have to discuss this. But what I'm wondering is, did you ever ask your sisters to treat Elliot like that, or to defend you in any way?"

TWENTY-FIVE

COLE

I slumped, eyes closed, waiting for the tightness around my chest to disband.

"Cole?" That was Gogo, with the small voiced that meant she'd taken Andi's words in her gut.

I paid attention to my breathing until I had the energy to speak. Looked my fill at Andi, who, back on the sidewalk, had gone and defused what had been turning into a bigass confrontation. Their diplomatic skills and ability to get along with everyone didn't always march so hand-in-hand. Sometimes it seemed like they put affability above every other consideration, but maybe that was part of their process, until they were more socially comfortable. Over the past couple of days of getting to know each other better, they'd been more relaxed. And more vulnerable. More willing to share that vulnerability not just with me, but with my family.

And now they'd seen past the surface of things, and in voicing their realization, plunged me into a conversation with my sisters that I'd been avoiding for years.

I'd decided it wasn't a battle I wanted to pick. Growing

up, they'd all occasionally gotten up in arms to protect or defend me, which, fair. I was a boy growing up in a body that didn't reflect that truth, and it wasn't always easy. It was Texas, after all. Even though it wasn't as dire, when I was growing up, as it currently was to exist as a trans person in Texas, I'd had my share of tense encounters. My sisters, once they knew who I was, always tried to make our little corner of the world safer for me.

And even once I was comfortable seeing to my safety— not because I'd added legal and medical transition to my social one, but because I was that much older and more confident—my family kept their guard up. I did my best to return the favor, but never told them to stop treating my every encounter with someone outside the family like it had the potential to devastate me.

So Andi's question about not speaking up? It hit me in the gut, too.

"I didn't ask them, no."

Both my sisters said my name, but I looked out the windshield instead of facing them.

I tried to speak with levity I wasn't feeling. "It's not the first time I've run into Elliot with them. It tends to go about like that. Not that I want to have long chats with the guy; he's been bratty since the breakup. Which was pre-pandemic, so you can imagine it's a bit tiring for him to still act that way."

Andi let out a brief laugh. "He probably thinks of it as part of his superhero origin story."

I took their hand again. We'd been staying connected like that since our first kiss. Quietly touching. Making room for each other. It grounded me as I went on, trying to explain the morass in my mind to Andi and to my sisters both.

"He probably does. Especially because if anyone from my family's around when we meet—and it's a small town, we meet pretty often—it turns into this nonsense battle scene. I only hope they don't do it when I'm not here."

Andi nodded. "So he sees y'all coming, and braces for a bunch of dismissive and cutting remarks from your sisters, who think they're protecting you. And you don't stop them because—this is my guess—you just want it over with and for you all to part ways. And afterwards, this small Texas town's queer community, if Elliot belongs to one, is probably hearing all about the intolerance of the Dunways. Who may have been great to you, specifically, during your transition, but who aren't earning any gold stars while picking a fight in front of the general public."

"We don't ... Cole, that's not—"

I turned on Margo then. "Intent and impact, Gogo. Which one matters?"

She bit her lips. "Fuck. Oh, fuck. Sorry."

Emmeline's head was down. I gave her a sec, then tapped her knee. "Emmers, sorry. That was a lot of noise. Is there anything you missed?"

She shook her head. We waited for her to look up. Her eyes were damp, and I felt like shit. But also: every one of these Elliot encounters had left me feeling like shit for so long, and I'd never figured out a way to explain it.

Not even to myself.

"We'll stop," Emmers said.

"Of course we will." Margo linked index fingers with Emmeline. "And apologize."

At that, Emmeline rolled her eyes, but she agreed. "Even though he is a snothead. And was even when you were dating."

I smiled a little. "He was fine. Mostly."

"Mostly fine. A ringing endorsement." There went Andi, resetting the temperature for us all again.

"Well, you never saw those postcards." Margo bit back a smile, and Emmeline snorted.

"You two are brats. Next time, don't read my correspondence."

"Next time, don't pin them to the fridge and let Sarita makes up a song from their words."

I flashed a look at Andi to see how they were taking this familial irreverence. And the evidence of my own past brattiness.

They raised their eyebrows. "Note to self: no sending you postcards."

I leaned over for a quick kiss. "Smart."

They held my gaze, and I held theirs right back, hoping they could see how I valued their intervention. Their eyes softened, taking on those same silvery depths I'd seen when we were on the water together.

I put on my Selena playlist and let it carry us home.

TWENTY-SIX

ANDI

After rising late, fucking around, walking on the beach with our coffee, and showering, I pulled out my laptop. Cole left me to my work, off to do more prep for the next day's big party at his family's house.

I did my job a little. It was two days until our four-day holiday weekend, so most of the place was pretty checked out, even those who seemed to still be in the actual office. The main thing I did, though, was wrap gifts for Cole's family. From the things I'd brought to Texas for Evelyn's family, I had scarves for three sisters, the travel scrapbook for Margo, and a set of bath bombs I hoped Larissa might appreciate more than Evelyn would have. That took care of his siblings, and I decided my feeling too awkward to come up with gifts for the rock stars meant I wouldn't give any of their partners anything.

In town, I'd picked up a sticker book for Alfie Junior and a squishy teething toy for the baby. I wrapped those, along with a digital photo frame for Cole's parents. Once I'd relabeled the gifts I'd brought from Philly, it made for a festive little pile on the coffee table.

And then there was my gift for Cole. He'd hampered the hell out of me, sticking so close and leaving me with little time to browse, until I'd evaded him at the bookstore. I'd found a set of recycled journals with thick, lie-flat pages and plain blue and purple covers. And stickers. There were so many vinyl stickers at the register; I'd spun the rack and grabbed a selection, hoping I had time to be discerning while also not running into any of the Dunways.

After some consideration, I affixed the kayak and spaceship to the purple notebook, and the rainbow, shorebird, and 'read banned books' ones on the blue. It didn't entirely make sense, but it also felt correct. Plus, I knew he'd like the colorful gel pens I wrapped with the journals. He seemed like a man who would get a lot out of it all. And if he took it as me being snide about his constant list-making and planning ... well. We were either okay with each other, or we weren't. The constant sex and touching—and occasional talks about some deep issues—suggested we were.

If I was wrong, if there wasn't space for me as I was, occasional snideness and all, then I may as well find out before I mistook the fun of making each other come with some kind of more momentous feeling.

The problem with momentous feelings being, as always, that it's dire if I'm alone in feeling them. And past experience didn't equate to future outcomes—maybe my feelings would plateau. Maybe Cole and I would come to feel equally intense about each other. Maybe all this was a flash in a forced-proximity pan. But if this wasn't one of those less likely scenarios, I could end up in that dire place I knew too well.

Alone, and far too vulnerable to the inner demon voices that told me I wasn't enough for anyone to want me for who I was. That it was better if I existed in solitude, playing nice so my found family wouldn't reject me outright, but not expecting anyone to make space for me when I let my friendly face fall.

Cole burst back into the cottage then, and the way he looked at me reminded me that, when I'd taken his family —and in a way, him—to task about Elliot, he'd appreciated it.

Appreciated it so much, he'd kept me squirming under his hands and tongue for ages.

"Are you cosplaying Santa?" He was wearing a red cap and had a black garbage sack slung over his shoulder.

"Yep. Want to be my elf?"

"Ew, no, power imbalance is not my kink."

"Speaking of." He set the sack down on the armchair and dug into it. "I meant to stop for this after lunch yesterday and got distracted by the whole family therapy in the car thing."

He passed me a drug store bag, in which I found lube, and ... "What part of your kink involves Reese's Pieces?"

He stopped nuzzling my neck to snatch the candy from me and toss it on the coffee table. "Oh, look at all your presents. You're too much."

"I'm really not. What did you bring besides chocolate?"

"More chocolate." He added another drug store bag to the table, then pulled out a bottle of wine and a cloth tote of groceries he set on the kitchen counter.

"Cole? You're up to something."

Instead of clarifying, he upended the rest of his bag, spilling a quilt and several cushions on the floor.

I caught my breath. "This ... isn't because you want to sleep on the sofa again, but needed it to be more comfortable."

He smirked and put the Santa hat on my head. "Nope.

Sarita and Ignatius told me more about your fic, how you do the holiday interludes, and last year was the crew making a blanket fort. It reminded me what you said at the airport about watching *The Muppet Christmas Carol* with your family."

"I told you that?"

"Well, you weren't super coherent, but I put the pieces together. So, I thought we could do that here. I know it's not the same ..."

His rare moment of uncertainty probably meant he was hoping this would please me. It maybe meant it mattered to him that I have a piece of my own holiday tradition down here, so far from where I'd thought I would spend Christmas.

"I like it."

He almost bounced with pleasure. "Excellent. I'm making us a charcuterie board. Is that okay for dinner, with popcorn and candy? I've got apples, so it's super healthy."

I slid the coffee table to rest under the window, away from my fort-building site. "Ha. So healthy. Dad used to make us grilled cheese sandwiches for fort time. Even Evelyn let that stand, though she added baby carrots and ranch dip to the menu."

"Sarita tried to add baby carrots to my grocery bag, but I wouldn't let her. She knows I can't stand them."

"There goes any hope I had that you and Evelyn could ever get along."

"My dreams, they are shattered." Cole moved the kitchen stools to the space beside the sofa. "But, Andi, seriously. I don't want to force this plan on you. I thought it would be—that it might be meaningful to you. And you've been so nice about being dragged into all my Christmas traditions. If you'd rather we, I don't know, go get some pizza or whatever, we can skip this. Just say the word."

TWENTY-SEVEN

COLE

I watched them carefully, feeling like some cross between a T-Rex and a mouse. Trampling all over Andi's past, but worried I'd stomped too far. Back at the house, with my family egging me on, it had seemed like a great idea. Brendan had even googled 'best foods to eat with *The Muppet Christmas Carol*,'—which, surprising us all, had a few hits—to come up with the menu for the evening.

None of that meant my plan was something Andi wanted. Them saying they liked it wasn't proof; they always defaulted to being agreeable. I wanted them to understand that they could be disagreeable if I was overstepping. Or for any other reason.

Their face was fully in neutral. "Are you trying to opt out because you think it's silly for me to be bent out of shape that I can't do this with Cass and Stell? Or is it because you don't actually want to get stuck under the fort with me?"

I wagged my eyebrows. "I'm all in favor of being stuck under blankets with you."

They shoved at my chest, but I found my balance by wrapping them in my arms.

"I want to opt in, Andi. If it's all right with you, sharing your tradition with me. I know it's not the same as doing it with your sisters, and I'm sorry you aren't getting that with them. And, no, I don't think your feelings are silly."

Their fingers playing at my nape made me lose my words, but since we were kissing again, I didn't think I needed to say much more to convince them of my sincerity.

Especially when they stepped back and said, "Go make me a feast. I have engineering to do. Are we watching on the TV or a laptop?"

"Whichever suits you. You don't need a hand?"

They hummed distractedly, and it was like the T-Rex and the mouse had skipped into the sunset together. They had all the sofa and chair cushions in one pile, the bed pillows in another. The sheets and blanket I'd used while sleeping on the sofa, the comforter from the bed, and a couple of beach towels ended up on the stripped-bare sofa, which Andi reversed so the back of it faced the TV console.

They didn't even notice me adding triangles of grilled cheese sandwiches to the trays of food I assembled.

After finishing in the kitchen, I checked out the impressive set-up. They'd rolled the edges of the rug and anchored them under the sofa, creating barriers to keep the cushions and pillows from overspilling, and tucked the comforter over the base as extra reinforcement. Several flat sheets were tucked into the sofa back and braced on the side chairs, leaving me an entrance tunnel between the stools.

It was chaotic and smart and perfect.

"Hang on, you've got to let me send pics to the family before I crawl in."

"Pass me the wine first."

I did, and Andi held it up, grinning, as I tried to capture the coziness and joy of it all with my camera.

"Oh, wait, let me out. There's another essential part of this whole thing."

They crawled forward, and I remembered to grab the lube, and candy, from the coffee table. We wouldn't want to forget anything essential. "What's that?"

"Pajamas. Only monsters would watch a blanket fort movie in day clothes."

I snickered. "Day clothes?"

They hip checked me after I helped them to stand. "You're the one intent on recapturing childhood magic for me here. Put up with my language."

"You got it. But can I wear sweats? I don't actually have pajamas."

"I've noticed." They leered back at me.

"I came here with a carry-on expecting to have this place to myself. Pajamas weren't necessary."

Andi tossed me a thermal undershirt printed with reindeers and sleighs. "You can wear that, since I don't think either part of my snow person PJ set will fit you."

"And sweats?"

"Or boxers, if you prefer. I don't suppose you have any winter themed ones? Or at least some green or red ones?"

They were so fucking cheerful, and even more so once I found I'd packed my blue and green check boxers. I wanted to keep giving them moments that made up for some of the crap they'd experienced when their stepmother denied them access to their sisters.

Throughout the movie—the grilled cheese was a little burned, but we devoured the rest of the main course, and only spent a little time tossing popcorn at each other—I kept thinking about those fancily wrapped gifts for Cassiopeia and Estella.

Partly cause I got so caught up in Kermit's Cratchit and Michael Caine's Scrooge that we never opened the lube. Not until the credits were rolling, and we began a bit of rolling of our own. The fort didn't stand up to our silliness. First the sheets came down on us, then the rug proved to be inadequate at containing the cushions.

My plaid boxers went missing in the jumble of blankets, though when Andi straddled me and stripped off their pajama top, they tugged my reindeer shirt back into place. I waggled my brows. "You have a thing for Dasher, or is it Dancer?"

"It's Blitzen. It's always been Blitzen." They ran their hands, light and teasing, over my shoulders and upper arms. "I was thinking."

I waited, tense and still through my torso but with restless legs aching to wrap round their hips. "What were you thinking?"

"About those sensitive nipples of yours." Their evil grin was the last warning I had before their mouth was on me, biting through the shirt with agonizingly thrilling directness. My body jerked. I moaned. They bit the other nipple and I clenched their hips, pressing so we could grind together.

The air between us was urgent, but also light. I wanted to strip them bare, not just of their festive pajamas, but of anything holding them back from me. Family baggage, worries about what would happen when we were back in Philly, whatever.

I flipped us so I could cradle their face as I kissed each feature. Gentle on their forehead, feathery on their cheeks and nose, intense when my lips found theirs.

"I give."

"Mm?" I hummed the question, busy nipping their earlobes and down their neck.

"That cushion just went sideways and now half my butt's on the floor. It's time to move this party to the bed."

TWENTY-EIGHT

ANDI

I grabbed the bed pillows. Cole snagged the water bottles and his drug store lube, because he was apparently determined to be penetrated. We were both naked by the time we made it to the bed, and I got caught up, again, in admiring his form. All the lean, dense muscle of him, and the dusting of dark hair across his chest, and, of course, his ass. I was so damn keen on Cole's ass.

He caught me looking and flexed, which made me sputter with glee.

I'd laughed so much since landing in this cottage with him. He'd seemed enchanted by the film—it was the one we always watched for a reason—and whenever my ungendered buddy Gonzo and his friend Rizzo the Rat were on screen, Cole's smiles sparked my own.

"Thanks for the movie night."

Cole rolled to his side to face me. We both sent hands roving over the other—a stroke here, a scraping of blunt nails there. The occasional squeeze, whenever my palm neared his butt.

"Thanks for your fort-building expertise. Sorry we destroyed it."

I grinned. "Nah, destroying it at the end is half the fun. Though I've never wrecked a fort in just that way before."

He played circles round my breasts. "I should hope not. I enjoy being part of upping the game some. Maybe even ..." He dipped his chin, grimacing a bit.

I walked my fingers up his chest and raked them through his beard. "Even?"

After a sigh, he kissed my palm. "Fine. Maybe even the start of a new kind of tradition. You don't have to remind me this is only the fourth night we've spent in this bed together—assuming you're not about to kick me out. I'm being a starry-eyed romantic or something. You can ignore it and just ... I don't know. Just let me go down on you until you're too exhausted to worry about my nonsense."

Fucking hell. Much as it had when he'd served me grilled cheese in our fort, my heart was doing a Kermit flail. It didn't feel safe.

I picked up the lube. Tried to be assertively sexy. Discovered the damn tube had one of those little silver foil seals over the opening, so I had to remove the cap, pry up the foil, and not lose every scrap of my vibe.

Cole's snickers weren't helping any. "So, I guess I didn't say too much?"

"Shush." It was hard to keep on a stern face when he took the foil and smushed it against the tip of his nose.

He wriggled that nose at me. "Because I get it if you don't want to have a big feelings talk. I mean, not just because we're in bed right now, but anytime."

My dry hand covered his mouth. My lubed hand covered his crotch. I narrowed my eyes. "Pay attention. I'm about to move one of my hands away, but I need you to stop blathering. Should I keep covering your mouth, or would you rather ...?"

I toyed my damp fingers against his entrance. His eyes slammed shut, and his body bowed between my two hands. He moaned.

"Thought so." I kissed him, letting my dry hand rest on his chest as I kept playing with his hole.

Cole propped one leg up, exposing more of himself to my exploration. When I buried one finger inside him, he moaned, but when I added a second, he stopped even trying to hold himself up. He spread eagle on the mattress, clutching at the sheets as I tongued first one nipple, then the other, into tightly furled peaks. I worked my way down his body, kissing rib by rib and relentlessly thrusting my fingers into him.

His dick glistened with need. I could practically see it pulsing as I neared, but it was the one part of him I left untouched. His abdominal muscles twitched as I explored them, his hips thrusting towards my mouth.

"Andi, you're killing me."

"Yep." I kept kissing his thighs, his stomach, the side of that butt I liked so much.

"Fine. If that's the game, fine. Come here." He sat up enough to slide my body perpendicular to his and reached for my core. It was my turn to moan. Cole opened himself fully to me again, but got a little distracted gauging my reactions to the way he teased my clit, tapping at the hood like I might deny him access.

I was pretty sure I was always going to allow Cole access.

His taps turned insistent and my kisses ramped up in return. We matched each other, me stroking my tongue down his dick and him circling my nub, somewhere between a race and a challenge to see who climbed the ramp to orgasm first.

Me. It was me. Cole wrenched his body away from my mouth and pinned me to the mattress, circling and tapping and rubbing and … just touching me so perfectly. So erotically. So very much in the way I needed to come.

And then I was the spread eagled one, catching my breath but letting my wits stay scattered. Especially once Cole loomed over me with questing hands and seeking tongue and ensured I was doubly, then triply satisfied with him.

"You?" I gathered myself to ask, and he snorted.

"Andi, you think I didn't fuck myself while I was going down on you? Don't you know me at all?"

Yeah. He had all the access.

I curled myself back onto the pillow, sure the smile I was beaming at him was sappy as hell. "Okay, well, if you, like, get horny again later, just let me know." I yawned, which may have taken a point or two off my credibility.

Cole linked our hands. "Yeah, I'll be sure to wake you up."

"Ha. Want me to go get the bedspread?"

"It's covered in popcorn and cheese, hon."

I snuggled closer to him. "I guess we only have each other for warmth, then."

"And the sheet." Cole nestled me into the crook of his arm. "Hey, on Saturday, how about we drive up to Clear Lake and deliver those gifts to your sisters?"

TWENTY-NINE

COLE

It was like I'd emptied my water bottle over Andi's head.

So much for cozy chats while we worked up the energy to wash up for sleep. They sat up and pulled on the reindeer shirt. "What?"

I tucked a pillow behind their back and draped the sheet over my lap. "It's the party tomorrow, so we don't really have time, plus I figured you might want to arrange the meeting first."

"We don't … have time. To spend six hours in the car, on the very minimal chance Evelyn wouldn't slam the door in my face. Because of your party."

I pressed my lips together. They weren't as enthused as I'd hoped. Not that I was admitting how spur of the moment my idea was. It might have emerged from several half-formed thoughts about Andi and family and traditions, but, also, it made the most sense.

We had flights home the day after Christmas, and would have to be at the airport early enough that stopping by Andi's stepmother's house wasn't workable. But we had down time between my family's party and Christmas Eve. And if Andi got to hand-deliver those sparkly boxes to their sisters, the drive time was worth it. "If you'd want to go tomorrow, we can. I don't need to be at our party on time. Or at all, really. I've seen the most important people already. If I miss out on awkward conversations with Aunt Max's son, that's a bonus."

Andi wasn't softening in the face of my more detailed plans and options. They climbed out of bed and tracked down their pajama pants, hauling them into the bathroom and shutting the door. I took the hint and fetched clean boxers and a t-shirt for myself. I also put fresh sheets on the bed and found a waffle weave blanket large enough to tuck in with hospital corners. I was sitting on top of the tidy bed when Andi emerged, freshly showered, and joined me.

They spoke like there'd been no pause in our talk. "Cole, Evelyn already said no."

"Right. You told me that. But you also told me she has her own family party on Saturday, so you'll know exactly where Estelle and Cassiopeia will be."

"Estella."

"Sorry, Estella. Someone likes astronomy names, huh?"

"Yeah, Dad did. He worked at NASA. Did I tell you that?" I shook my head.

"He was an aerospace engineer. So, yeah. Andromeda, Estella, and Cassiopeia, his three stars. I wasn't even the only Andromeda in my elementary school, which is what happens when you live in a community with a bunch of rocket scientists."

It was a lot of openness from them, a lot of wistful remembrance. I didn't want to spoil the mood again; didn't want to do my T-Rex stomp over their stories about the father they'd lost.

Or, rather, I did. I wanted to push my idea to ambush their stepmother, because fuck that woman for denying Andi time with their family. Andi was a damn treasure of a person, and they deserved as much contact with the star-name girls as they wanted.

Look at how they'd given me the language to confront my family. During party prep, every one of my sisters had pulled me aside to apologize and tell me they understood the difference between supporting me and punching down at others. Margo had sent me a whole-ass notes app paragraph expressing the family's remorse and vows to do better for me to send on to Elliot.

That was all because of Andi. Giving them a bowl of popcorn and a few orgasms wasn't near thanks enough. I wanted to give them the family they longed to see.

"That's nice, that you're linked like that to your sisters."

"Don't get me wrong, I've disliked my given name since before I knew I disliked being forced into a gender binary. I've been Andi my whole life. Well, obviously, but you know what I mean. It was a thing I learned to articulate when I was young." They shrugged. "Dad was casual about it. About most things, really. I think that's why I never had to articulate anything about my gender expression, not until Evelyn came along and wanted me to fit into a box. I was in middle school then, anyway, so I'm sure if Evelyn didn't force me to define myself, my peers would have."

"Your dad accepted your definition, though?"

Andi shifted to lean back against the headboard. "Yeah. He wanted me to be pragmatic about it. Pick my battles. Remember who I am inside doesn't change no matter what others say about me, blah blah. He did side with Evelyn when she said Stell and Cass had to be ten before I asked them to use my pronouns. I guess that was more of him being pragmatic."

"Yikes." I squeezed their knee. "I mean, their words don't matter, blah blah."

They huffed a laugh. "Right. Well. Evelyn gets her wish now, since Dad's not around to model acceptance."

"Hang up. How old are your sisters now?" I'd guessed they were still smalls, but if they were in double digits, my T-Rex plan would probably work even better.

"Ten and twelve. But seven and nine when Dad died, so still inside Evelyn's 'nonbinary people are too confusing' timeframe."

I edged closer. Kissed their shoulder. "You're not too confusing."

"Yeah, yeah, blah, blah."

"Do they have cell phones?"

"The girls?"

I nodded.

"I don't know. Probably Estella does?"

"Do they know your number?"

Andi shrugged, but it was a more hunched into themself shrug than before. I was stomping again.

"I'm going to shower." It was an abrupt break in the conversation, but necessary so I could contain the T-Rex impulses. When I got back to the bedroom, Andi was tucked in on their side, with just my lamp still lit.

"I started a load of sheets washing."

"Thanks. Are these turned back covers a signal I can join you?"

Their smile glowed, even in the low light. "They are. But before you try to swoop in and run my life with your 'Cole always has to control the plan' ways, can you just ... let it go?"

I settled myself onto the mattress beside them, covering my flash of disappointment with my movement. "Fair. And yes, I can."

I talked about the Muppets, and we ranked other good Christmas movies, and it was good. It wasn't 'together we will scheme to take down Andi's foes and leave naught but rubble—and some thoughtful presents—in our wake' good, but it was better, by a huge margin, than sleeping on the sofa.

CHAPTER

THIRTY

ANDI

I woke up seething. It was a problem.

I kept fixating on all the reasons I'd balked about following Cole to his hometown in the first place—his bossy conviction he knew how to fix any situation, the way I'd have to fit in with a bunch of strangers, the weight of missing Stell and Cass untempered by the coping mechanisms I'd created in my normal life.

Cole was relaxed in sleep, unbothered by anything. Well, as far as I knew, unbothered. I slid out of bed instead of continuing to lie beside him, casting aspersions on his indifference. It was an unfair accusation for my erratic mind to come up with. If he'd been more indifferent to my problems, he wouldn't keep proposing outlandish solutions.

I changed over the laundry. Blanket forts always left me with a lot of laundry, but I'd come to like the process of getting everything put back in order. Sweeping up the food crumbs, and fluffing the sofa cushions, and squaring the coffee table on the rug. Cleaning up at Cole's beach cottage involved more sand than I was used to, and less of a sense

124

that the restored living room held a dose of holiday magic. But the tidiness still settled a bit of my soul.

Cole emerged in time to help me fold. "Hi."

I passed him the fitted sheet. "Hi to you. Coffee's ready."

He nodded. "Smells great. And the room looks great. You didn't have to do all this alone."

I pulled another flat sheet from the basket. "It's fine. It's kind of meditative. I mean, I'm not as routine about cleaning at home as I could be, except for looking after Moscato. But that's daily stuff. This is ..."

"Part of the tradition?" He asked once I'd trailed off for too long.

"Yeah."

We folded the last flat sheet together.

Over breakfast, Cole took a deep breath, like he was bracing for something. My guards were already half-up when he blurted, "Do you sing?"

"I ... what?"

"I mean, in front of others, not just along with the radio. And no one cares if it's good, but tonight, at the party, people will sing Christmas songs. Some as singalongs, whoever wants joins in, but individuals do, too. I want to be sure we have the music for you, if you want to perform."

Goddamn Dunway Christmas extravaganza. Tamales and tins of cookies and blinking multicolored lights and custom cocktails and now singalongs, too? People would probably show up to this party in ugly holiday sweaters, even though the temps would barely be in the fifties.

"You want me to get up there with Brendan Brody and Scorch Madigan and warble about Rudolph?"

He snickered. "I know you said you're hot for Blitzen, but maybe we shouldn't share that with my entire extended family."

I tossed my napkin at him.

"Seriously, though, it's low key. No one judges quality or anything. And if you don't want to join in, there's no pressure. You can even absent yourself entirely, like Emmeline does."

"Does she even like the party?"

Cole's half-smile was so full of affection. "Nope. She'll spend as much of it as she wants to attend in the backyard and then slip off to her room whenever she's tired of it all."

"Maybe I'll just see if she wants to hang down here with me tonight."

"And, what? Not go? I told you, you don't need to sing."

"Sure, but it's not like I'm a planned guest. Look, you've included me in a bunch of your family time, which has been kind, but I've taken you away from them a lot, too. That wasn't your plan when you used an entire week of vacation days to come down here. I've got some work I can do, and writing if I want, or I can binge a rewatch of *Our Flag Means Death*. There's no need to drag me along and have to explain who I am to a bunch of people I'll never see again."

He stood and gathered our plates. I took a moment to center myself.

"I didn't mean that you're dragging me." I might not have even meant I'd never see them again. Not that I'd admit that.

Cole looked like he wished the sink was across the room, so he could wash the dishes with his back to me. Too bad for him. He finally shut off the water and dried his hands. "I know you didn't. Or, I know you mostly didn't, but also, you kind of did."

I squinted, but it still made little sense. "Okay? Explain." Because it sounded like he was going to tell me about the best way to live my life again, and it was barely ten hours from when I'd specifically asked him to not do that.

He followed me to the sofa, which was rapidly losing any of the dang happy holiday memories. "Andi, I feel like you're retreating from me. I mean, if you're looking for ways to distance yourself from my family? I get it. I know we're a lot, especially everyone all at once, and you have your thing where you always have to get along with everyone, which I'm sure is exhausting after a while."

I could feel my face flaming, but if it was temper or embarrassment, I wasn't sure. Hopefully temper, because I didn't want Cole Dunway, or anyone, defining 'my thing' to me. And even less did I want him hitting on my issues with any accuracy. "My thing? Where I do what, exactly?"

THIRTY-ONE

COLE

I rubbed my neck. If I'd taken more than a minute to figure out my desired outcome of this conversation, I'd probably not have started with accusing Andi of being a people pleaser. It was their coping mechanism, and instead of respecting that, I'd framed it as an issue.

"I'm sorry. It's not any of my concern."

"No, but you brought it up, anyway. So now I want you to explain that, too."

Relaxing against the sofa, in hopes it prompted some mirroring and us both letting go of some tension, I looked them in the eye. "Hon, you are great at peopling. I knew that the day we met, that your friendliness makes you someone everybody likes. But even extroverts don't want to be on all the time, and you haven't had a ton of space for yourself since we got here. Especially since ..."

I found myself staring at the bedroom, probably smiling too much, because Andi's voice was sharp when they asked, "But that's not what you said, is it? You didn't say I'm friendly, or even that I'm too friendly. You said I have to get along with people, like it's a compulsion. And not a healthy one."

At least I'd stopped myself from protesting that their affability wasn't the point. "I know, I'm sorry. Look, I don't, absolutely do not, think it's an issue, or a compulsion, or unhealthy. None of that. I think it's a tool you use in new situations. We all have tools like that, armor we put on when we need it. You've mentioned my trying to control things a time or two, right? But I shouldn't have made it sound like a problem. Especially since you've shown me—shown my sisters, even—how great you are when you shed that armor and let me know more of the person you are inside."

They were on their feet. I scrambled to join them on the patio, where they sat to put on their shoes. "Do you need away from me, or can this be a walk for two?"

Andi took a deep breath. "For two. I want to move, I want the ocean air, and I want to not sit there listening to you talk yourself deeper into a hole."

I grimaced. "Fair. So fair."

We set off around the side of the cottage and down the boardwalk to the beach. The breeze picked up as soon as we hit the dunes, and I passed Andi a hoodie.

"Thanks."

"Of course."

We strolled for a bit. Other than identifying a couple of Royal Terns on the beach, I stayed quiet.

Andi didn't, not for long. "I think you felt like I solved the Elliot problem, which you couldn't solve on your own, and that threatened your bossiness, which is your armor, and that's why you started harping on my relationship with my family."

After blurting all that out, Andi pulled up the hood and kept their gaze on the ocean for several steps.

I looked only at the sand.

And thought. And felt. And thought some more. "Oh, crappity crap crap."

Andi stopped walking. "What?"

I scrubbed my hands over my face. "You heard me."

"I mean, I did. I'm not sure what you meant, but I heard you." Their arms circled my waist, and I touched my forehead to theirs. It was our first hug of the day, which was a perfect time to realize I'd been counting hugs.

I swallowed hard. "So, yeah. That was me conceding your point. I'm still grateful to you, because I needed your intervention about Elliot, and my sisters did, too. You were perceptive, and also fairly kind in how you call us out. But apparently, I can be thankful and a pushy jerk at the same time."

They kissed me, light and sweet, and I breathed easier. They said, "Not quite a jerk. Maybe not as introspective as you could be. And sometimes, maybe, you approach things as problems you can solve, instead of wondering if you're the one that needs examining."

It was a lot to take in, but their words also settled into some crevices inside me I hadn't noticed needed filling. "Good thoughts. Yeah. Okay. So first off, I'll stop harping about your family. For real this time. And I officially retract what I said about you pulling away, too. That was more of me getting bossy, I guess."

Their smile was a tad impish. "Well. You weren't entirely wrong about my armor. As you may have noticed from the fact that we're on the beach instead of in the cottage, I like to retreat sometimes."

I had to kiss them. It was my favorite new compulsion. "Turns out we're both wise. That's handy."

"Especially when we combine it with being willing to listen to each other?"

Yeah, more kisses were essential. After a long, delicious moment, I asked, "Interested in messing up another set of sheets with me?"

Andi's laugh startled an oystercatcher into taking flight. They took my hand and led the way back up the beach. "I am, but first, I'm going to call Evelyn and tell her we're coming to see my sisters."

THIRTY-TWO

ANDI

Estella answered her mom's phone. Cole must have felt me freeze up, cause he unwrapped himself from my torso and brought me a box of tissues and a glass of water. A quick squeeze to my shoulder, and he went to deal with the next load of laundry.

I found him in the bedroom a few minutes later, when I walked in, saying, "Hang on, little star, let me get a pen."

Cole passed over my backpack from the dresser behind him, making wide, hopeful eyes at me. I couldn't guess what my expression told him in return, but I tried to hold a smile for him while I dug out my notebook.

"Okay, ready." I copied down the phone number Estella recited. "Got it. I'll text you right now. No, listen, it's okay. I promise, it doesn't matter. All that matters is figuring it out, and look at us now, figuring. We're so on top of this."

Cole cleared away the clean blankets and leaned the pillows against the headboard, making a little nest for me beside him. I sank to join him, listening to my sweet, bright, silly sister's words. The whole time I told her we were fine, and that I'd talk to her and Cass soon, and swore I wouldn't leave Texas until we'd seen each other, Cole sat beside me, letting me grip his thigh to make sure I was present in this new reality.

Even after I hung up, still and unfocused and quiet, he just held space for me until I was up to talking.

"That was Estella. Evelyn had the food processor going, so she didn't even see it was me calling. She said who she was talking to; it's not like I'd have told her to lie to her mom."

"I know."

It wasn't even a big part of what was in my head, but his complete acceptance of that tiny statement somehow kicked my gears back online. I dragged in a breath full of the cool ocean air that lingered even when we were shut away inside the cottage. Shook my head. "So, yeah. You were right, by the way. She got a phone for her birthday, but all the times she's asked about it, Evelyn's kind of ignored her asking for my number. I mean, she probably didn't ask daily or anything. She's still a tween. But still. I have her contact now. Oh, hang on."

I texted my sister. Stared at my phone for the fifteen seconds it took for her to reply. I felt the kind of smile that might end up being indelible grow and take root.

"That's amazing." Cole kissed my temple.

"I know, right? It's hard to grasp."

"So, what about our trip? Are we on for tomorrow?"

I wilted. "Yeah, no. Evelyn's family moved their party to today, and tomorrow morning they all leave to spend a few nights in Ft. Worth with the boyfriend's family. They're not back until Wednesday."

And Cole and I were leaving for Philly on Tuesday.

"Are they driving? Is there any chance they'd push back their departure, do you think? Or come back early?"

I huffed out a breath. "Stell asked her that. I mean, maybe she and Cass together can talk her round, but it seemed like a pretty firm no, from what I could hear."

"Well, shit."

"Yep." I squeezed my eyes shut to get myself back under control. Sniffed, and ignored how that didn't leave me feeling too appealing. Because I wanted Cole to know how much he appealed to me. I swung myself around to straddle him.

He raised his brows. "Hi."

Goof of a man. "Hi. Thanks for respecting my need to have that call on my own."

He laughed a little. "I mean, you're welcome. But if that's where your bar is, I have a feeling I'm going to get away with a lot while we're together."

That smile bloomed again. "While we're together?"

His hands tightened on my hips. "You didn't think I was living this thing between us only in the present, did you? Andi, I've already mapped out the fastest ways to get from my place to yours depending on if it's a weeknight or weekend. Does your complex have a parking garage, by the way? Do you have rules for who can use visitor spaces? I couldn't tell from their website."

"Damn, friend, you are eager." And a bit too into controlling every facet of his life, but we didn't need to revisit that talk just yet.

His face sobered by a couple of degrees. "Too eager?"

I shook my head. "Definitely not. I mean, I haven't added your address to my favorites yet, but mostly that's because you haven't given it to me."

"Are you sure? Because it's on the contact card I sent you back at Jerome's Thanksgiving brunch."

Goofy, controlling goof of a man. I kissed him, even if

my nose was too sniffly. Pulling back, I threaded my hands through his hair. "You're in my future, too, Cole. I ... maybe we're too pulled out of our normal time and place here, this week, but. Yeah. I'm pretty sure I'd not be getting so upset about things, and retreating, and all the rest, if I didn't feel pretty deeply already that it's important for you and me to learn to communicate with each other. For a big, long time."

He tumbled me to our sides, throwing a thigh over my legs and pressing our bodies as completely together as we could get while still clothed. "Andi. Fuck. I'm so gone over you. I'm going to be the one crying now."

We hugged tight, the air between us quietly full of the buzz of intense and happy emotions. It meant the world, just then.

THIRTY-THREE

COLE

After the most peaceful of moments, Andi spoke into my shoulder. "I'm going to head north now and track down the girls. I don't know how else I'll get to see them. It's still okay if I use the car?"

I nodded against their head. "We can drive up together. Pack for an overnight, in case the tracking down takes a while. Or in case you get a lot of time with them, so we don't have to be driving back too late. Not speaking for you, but I've been sleeping less than normal, what with all the other fun I've been having in bed."

Andi pulled away. "Cole, no. Your party."

I scoffed. "It's not that big a deal."

They sat up then, grabbing their phone and tapping for a moment. "Right. Here it is. And I quote, 'The biggest event other than Christmas Day is Friday's Dunway Family Party.' So, yeah, it seems like a big deal."

I extracted their phone and set it aside. "I wrote big event, not big deal. It's a lot of moving parts, and we did a lot to put it together, with the light display and the tamales and all. Mopping the kitchen twice, cause as soon as I finished, Alfie Junior trekked through eating one of those yogurt pouches and he slipped on the floor and it went everywhere. He's fine, by the way."

"I figured, otherwise, you'd have led with that."

"Right." I nodded. "So now everything's set up, and I already spent time with the important people while we got ready. Tonight is just all the extras: friends of the elders, the more distant relatives. Aunt Max's annoying son. No one I need to have the same conversation over and over with, you know? Let one of my sisters tell them all that yes, I'm happy with my new job and yes, I enjoy living in Philly, and yes, I'm happy to be back with everyone for the holiday."

The more I talked about it, the greedier I was for an out from the whole thing. Andi didn't seem at all convinced, though. They were looking everywhere but at me. Fidgeting with the hem of the pillowcase. Hitching their breath when their gaze landed on the gifts for their sisters.

I gestured at their phone. "You've put up with a lot from that dossier of mine already. And when we get back, there's still more togetherness. The big meal before the church goers head to midnight services. A silly amount of hoopla about Spencer's first Christmas. Dueling baked French toast recipes to argue about. That's Brendan and Alfie Senior's thing, by the way. I didn't put it on the schedule, but they've got this rivalry going, and they will absolutely serve you a double portion without telling you who made which, and then demanding you declare a winner. So, see? There's more than enough Dunway nonsense for us both. It'd be unfair for you to do all this with my family and not have me involved in some tiny way with your own."

They made the most screwed-tight face. "Yeah, I don't think fairness has been much of a factor in my family holiday. Not much of a factor in any of my holidays since Dad passed, but. Well. I'm trying to … recapture, I guess, some of what I need at Christmas. And that means seeing Estella and Cassiopeia, even if it's only for half an hour. But it's ridiculous for you to spend six hours driving and missing time with your people just so I can hug my sisters."

I was restraining every one of my bossy urges. Or trying to, at least. Probably it wasn't much to congratulate myself on, that I hadn't already packed our toothbrushes and texted my family chat that I'd see them all tomorrow. "Andi, can I please go with you? Because I don't think it's ridiculous. I think helping you to get those hugs is the most important thing I could possibly do. And we don't know exactly what'll happen when we get there, how easy it'll be to reach them. You might have to drive around, you might have to be on your phone with Estella while y'all figure it out. Let me be the chauffeur, and your distraction if you need one, and the polite stranger standing beside you if that means your stepmother would feel awkward being rude to your face. Please, can I?"

They side-eyed me. "Very sneaky of you to offer that polite stranger argument."

I did not grin, because I knew how to keep my victory celebrations low key. "I mean, it seems, from how you've described her, that it might make a difference."

"It's like you've met suburban Texan women before."

Okay, I did grin. "That's a yes?"

"First, you have to see if your parents mind."

"They don't." I found my phone and messaged everyone.

"You haven't given them time to reply." But for all their chiding, Andi was already standing at the dresser, making minute adjustments to the ribbon on the presents. Making them even more perfectly pretty, even though they were bound to get a little mussed during our drive.

I gathered my toiletry kit and dropped it in the bottom of a big tote bag people used to haul towels and stuff down to the beach. I added a change of clothes and left it by the door, carrying my phone to Andi to show them the string of encouragement from my parents and sisters. "Mama says we need to swing by the house on the way out to grab a tin of Christmas cookies for your stepmother."

They checked my screen and shook their head at me. "You are ... It's very easy to see how you became exactly who you are, Cole Dunway."

It was, in a way, the most precious statement about me they'd made all day.

THIRTY-FOUR

ANDI

Cole's sister texted me when we were an hour out from Clear Lake. "You gave my number to Margo?"

He turned down the music, which he'd kept on a playlist heavy on Scorch Madigan and Brendan Brody songs. Claimed it was some kind of solace for the fact I was missing the rockers singing Christmas songs, but I suspected it was really another way of distracting me. Settling me into some kind of pumped up vibe. The occasional Dolly Parton and Beyonce songs only confirmed my suspicions. Any second now, *Toxic* would slide into our soundscape.

"Is that okay? I figured that way they can get ahold of one of us if they need anything. What's she saying?"

"Nothing. She's being supportive. It only surprised me to hear from her."

He took my hand over the console. "You might have to get used to it. She's not going to blow up your phone as much as Jerome does, but Gogo's chatty."

"I think that's just how she is with you. And Karl, I guess."

Cole screwed up his lips. "Hmm. It's not the first time someone said she and I are notably close."

"It's nice. I hope Stell and Cass are as close as you and your sister when they're grown."

The way his hand tightened on mine made me listen back to my own words. I did that, sometimes. Discounted my potential importance to my sisters.

I sighed. "I was fifteen when Estella was born. I love them more than anyone, but it's never going to be like you and Margo. Or even you and ... which sister are you least close to?"

Cole's face was priceless. "I don't—"

"I'm not asking you to put one of them up for sale. But you've got five sisters, and only Margo is your best friend. There's got to be one that you don't vibe with as much. Is it Larissa, since she's the biggest age gap?"

"No. And the gap's the same with Emmers."

"So it's Jeannie."

He shot me a glare, but I squeezed his hand.

"I like every one of your sisters, Cole. They can text me as much as they want. But you can't tell me it's likely I'll ever be as close to mine as you are to any of yours. Or that they'll be as close to me as the two of them are to each other. They were too young to remember the years I lived with them full time, and even though we can talk more often now, it's not going to be the same as all the shared experiences they'll have with each other."

And on top of all that, my sisters were being raised by Evelyn. Who'd brought an even more conservative person than she already was into their lives. I didn't know the boyfriend, but expected he and Evelyn would happily continue to dismantle Dad's groundwork. I didn't quite expect to be told I was a dangerous influence to be around children, but if they sneered, if they insisted on gendering me until it was easiest for my sisters to go along with it? It wouldn't surprise me.

"Cole?"

"Andi." He smiled at me.

I switched off the music. Tucked my restless fingers under my thighs. "When we get there—if we manage to see them. They're going to make a point of calling me 'young woman' or something. Not my sisters; Evelyn and whoever she has around her. And I'm going to seethe internally, and maybe you will, too, but …"

"But let it go? It's not the right battle to pick?"

"Right. That." My smile trembled. "Sorry."

"Hon. It's not my business to tell you which battles you opt in to. I'm only happy you're letting me take arms at your side for the ones you choose."

This guy. The way he'd actively reined in his take-chargeness to follow my lead shouldn't be so touching. I wasn't the crusader Cole was; far more often, I was the person who allowed themself to fit inside other's expectations. The one who minimized interpersonal friction and found ways to accept my lot in life.

So I got why people like Cole sometimes thought I was spineless. Cole himself had never treated me that way, but he wasn't the only bossy person I knew. And those others? Yeah, they were more than ready to share their opinions with words like 'passive' and 'steamrolled' and even 'self-loathing.'

Which I was not.

Did I value getting along with my chosen community more than I valued asserting myself? Probably. But I needed that community. I needed, for so many reasons essential to my well-being, to have a place where I could count on being welcomed, and accepted, for the genderqueer introverted dreamer I was.

The kind of space Cole had made for me, back in his beach cottage. That his family had, too, in their slightly chaotic but always welcoming way. It almost had me looking forward to the rest of my time with the Dunways. Almost had me prepared to endure my stepmother.

My phone dinged, and this time, the text was from my sister.

My sister. Texting me. Of all the Christmas miracles.

"It's a selfie." I flashed the screen at Cole, even though we were on the freeway, so he had no chance to take it in. Besides, I wanted to soak in the details of Stell and Cass making goofy, put-upon faces for the camera. "They're being hustled into their party clothes. Oh, God, are those dresses velvet? They're going to roast alive."

"It is unseasonably cold."

"Yeah, but it's not, like, Scotland, which is the way Evelyn imagines the wintertime, no matter the weather. All flocking and gingham and cobblestone streets, somehow. She puts on the AC if she has to, just so she can wear sweaters from Thanksgiving to New Year's."

He winced. "Sorry to the planet, and also to everyone living in her world."

"Seriously. Okay, so." I stopped zooming in on my sisters' faces to read the texts. "It seems like they're on their way out the door soon. It'll take them maybe half an hour to get to Evelyn's brother's place. Should I tell her we're on the way?"

Cole blew out a breath. "Does her mom read her texts?"

"I mean, probably. It's in keeping for her to have a

parental control set up. Which is probably good parenting, I don't know. Anyway, I think it's better to keep the element of surprise, and that social pressure of her having to be polite in front of everyone. Let's grab something to eat and make our battle plan."

THIRTY-FIVE

Andi's nerves had them bouncing in the booth across from me.

"Hey." I covered their forearm with my palm. "This is going to work. We maybe will have to get through some bullshit first, but come on. You and me? We've survived lots of bullshit in our lives, and are sitting here in this festively decorated Salvadorian restaurant, living our hard-won and excellent truths."

Andi made a considering face. "Are these pupusas, like, a reward for survival?"

"Don't know about yours, but mine sure are. Have you tried the loroco yet?"

They nodded. "You have a point. Okay, we're going to survive. I choose to believe."

"Survive and thrive, hon. And," I smoldered at them. "Once we're done triumphing, I booked us a king room in one of the most highly coveted mid-range highway-adjacent hotels in the area. So prepare to be utterly swept away."

Andi threw their head back, laughing, which was the best sight imaginable.

Their cheer lasted as we made our way to their step-uncle's house. They sang—with more gusto than skill, but also without apology—along with the choruses of several songs. They refreshed their topknot and ran an approving hand over their rainbow-hued undercut. They were calm and matter-of-fact, pointing out Evelyn's car parked on the street as we approached our destination.

"You'll take pictures of me with them, even if it's a fleeting moment?"

"I will. I promise. I've got my camera set on 'live' so you'll have lots of frames to choose from."

"I'm taking the presents with me. In case."

I nodded. Affirming every plan, standing beside them as they approached the door. I gave them every support I could think up.

A man in a shirt printed with holly berries answered the door. From Andi's demeanor, they were not anybody on my personal shit list. Especially since he immediately stood back to let us in, introducing himself to me as if our showing up at this doorstep wasn't notable.

A few people in the house greeted Andi, and a few more turned towards an interior room as soon as they saw us. It made it easy enough to guess that that's where we would find at least one of the people who we sought. We followed the looks into a formal dining room, discovering a laden table and several adults, but no children. Andi approached a statuesque woman in a red and gold plaid sweater with faux fur accents. She flared her nostrils, but sounded as pleasant as can be when she said, "Andromeda, dear, you made it," as if this was very much the plan.

Andi had their most social smile fixed in place as they leaned in for a half-hug. "Merry Christmas, Evelyn."

I stepped in then, intent on buying some time for Andi to find the girls. "Hi, Cole Dunway. I've heard so much about you. Been looking forward to meeting you in person."

I shot a conspirator's grin at Andi, tipping my chin in a subtle suggestion they go in search of their sisters. I took the tin from them and turned back to Evelyn. "We brought you a selection of our family's Christmas cookies." Without giving Evelyn time to react, I launched into a description of the types we baked, and the way we decided that iced oatmeal counted as a Christmas cookie even though it wasn't as traditional as the sugar cookies or the gingerbread Santas, and a rundown of exactly which ones were gluten-free and how my oldest sister had sources snowman-patterned cupcake liners to segregate the gluten-free cookies from the other cookies, which were nestled in red and green and gold paper, instead.

It was inane chatter, but I made enough eye contact with the others in the room to draw them into my conversation, and, as I'd hoped, Evelyn stuck around to listen while Andi roamed the house. Next thing I knew, I heard happy squeals. Andi returned to the dining room with their arms around their sisters. I was already taking pictures as they crossed the threshold, and Andi grinned and held them in place to pose.

All three were giggling, and Andi's eyes shone. And I'd have driven us five times as many miles to get this moment for them.

The younger sister—Cassiopeia—dashed to hug her mom. "You didn't tell us Andi was coming to the party! This is the best ever."

We all moved to a corner of the room, where someone

had set the dining chairs against the wall, presumably for easier access to the food table. Evelyn smoothed her daughter's hair. "It's lovely to see your sister."

Andi's lips pressed tight for a moment, but they didn't protest the gendered term. I offered a wincing shrug, and they lowered their shoulders a fraction. They introduced me to the girls, which gave me the chance to unhook the tote bag with the gifts from their shoulder.

Andi's eyes shone at the reminder. "Oh! Hey, Stell, Cass. Here."

The girls, almost at the same time, draped the snowflake tulle ribbons over their shoulders like scarves, before opening the gifts. I stepped back and took pictures so I could capture their grins, as well as Evelyn's grimace. It also let me cover my smirk.

From the boxes, they pulled some art stuff and some tech stuff, but the clear stars of the gifts were the photo books. Each one had a pic of the three siblings on the cover, dressed in winter-themed sweaters and cuddled up around a man who was clearly their dad. Quiet descended between them all as the sisters leafed through the pages, nudging each other to share images of blanket forts, of Christmas mornings with wrapping paper everywhere, of all of them piled in the back seat of a car in front of houses with fuse-blowing amounts of light displays. I only saw a few of the pages over everyone's shoulders, but it seemed Andi had interspersed years of photos with a lot of text. Clearly, they'd used their storytelling skills to enhance the memories of holidays with their dad.

Evelyn took a stack of gilt napkins off the dining table and handed them around to blot everyone's eyes. When she passed one to Andi, she said, "The books are lovely. And thoughtful. Thank you."

Andi bit their lip a sec, then nodded. "I miss him, too, you know."

"I know. Of course I know. I ..." She looked away, fixing on a false smile as she waved to someone in the other room. "It's good you came by."

After that concession, it took only a few minutes of tween pleading, location sharing, and letting Evelyn take a photo of my driver's license, before the Ennis siblings got permission for us to spend an hour driving around to look at Christmas lights.

THIRTY-SIX

ANDI

Cole interrogated Evelyn's sister-in-law about the best nearby light displays while the rest of us bundled into our coats and reassured Evelyn.

What I loved most about that was his newly revealed ability to step back and leave me in charge of negotiating with my stepmother.

Not that he'd lost his need to control all kinds of facets of the world. As we approached the car, he mapped a route that took us via a Starbucks for hot chocolate, surveyed Stell and Cass about their music preferences, and asked if I wanted to sit in the back between my sisters. If I wasn't so overwhelmingly buzzed about everything, I might even have objected to his once again taking charge. For the record, if for no other reason.

But Dad's three stars were orbiting together again, and I wasn't complaining about anything.

We found our way to one of those neighborhoods with a few heavily decorated blocks, and Cole parked so we could walk around a couple of them. Cass wore the LED gloves I'd just given her, and Cole took video of us dancing

150

to the tinny *Jingle Bells* playing over one house's sound system, Cassiopeia's glowing, multicolored fingers flying as we twirled each other around.

It wasn't nearly enough, but it was infinitely more time with them than I'd resigned myself to having. By the time we dropped them back with Evelyn—once again successfully avoiding meeting her date—my jaw hurt from smiling.

Back outside, I tackle-hugged Cole like I was one of my giddy tween sisters. He missed not one beat, swooping me into a spin and nuzzling my neck until I squirmed away from his ticklish beard.

"Hey, there."

"Hi back at you." I squeezed him before stepping back to take his hand as we walked to the car. "I was going to offer to drive, but I think I'm too distractible just yet. Know what's silly?"

"What's that?"

"Between us, we have seven sisters."

"We sure do."

"It's just ... So. Many. Sisters."

He nudged his shoulder to mine. "It definitely is. Good thing we found our way to our true genders, else that would have been too many sisters altogether."

I held our linked hands in the air, triumphant. "Go us, queering our way past an excessive amount of sisterhood."

He laughed. "I like this lightness for you."

And then Cole held the car door open for me, which made me growl and drag him around to the driver's side, so I could open the door for him, instead. "Don't be chivalrous at me."

"Sorry, sorry. I meant nothing by it. I'm just in a hurry

to get us on the way to our hotel, so we can get ourselves naked."

I shoved a little to propel him into his seat, then circled around to my own. "Just for that, I'm not kissing you again until we're in our room."

It was an idle threat, given how I was still more lit up than the house we'd just seen, with the icicle lights hanging off each eave and the lawn display of Santa's workshop full of a dozen elves. But he didn't call me on it. Not even when I dragged his mouth to mine at the first red light we came to.

He did laugh, but that was fair enough.

The hotel was as generic as promised, like the inverse of how much charm the beach cottage had. But we weren't in it for the bland carpeting and blander wall art. We were in it to fuck.

I shrugged off my coat—too heavy for Houston, but I hadn't packed anything else—and shoved down my nice jeans. Worked loose each shirt button with fumbling fingers. Cole was stripping with a less frantic air, but his eyes stayed on mine. Capturing me with his calm intensity. With his warmth. With his way of projecting that what mattered to him was to be a solid, confident, supportive presence in my life.

I plastered myself to him and tumbled us onto the bed.

His face glowed up at me. "I guess we're turning in early? It's not even ten."

"Hush." I kissed him. He soon broke free to trail his lips across my shoulders and down the center of my chest. All these sure-handed touches and heat-seeking kisses that proved how well we'd come to know each other's minds and bodies and selves over the week of intimacy.

I ran my hands through his hair, scraped fingernails at his back as his mouth found my core. Spread my legs to keep him close as he explored and nipped and tasted. Arched my back.

Cried out my release.

Also, a little bit, I cried.

My tears didn't stream down my cheeks for long, between my internal fight for control and the way Cole cradled my face. His whole length stretched over mine, somehow both holding me and rocking me in place, and it was a total balm.

"Big day."

I nodded a little, deep-breathing the comfort of his scent and mine mingled together. "You doing okay?"

"I'm doing the best."

I couldn't stop myself from wrinkling my nose. "Pretty sure I'm the one that just orgasmed, not you."

"Yeah, but I got to play with you until you came. Which is my favorite thing to do. So I stand by my statement."

It was the sweetest of sentiments, but also? We were getting really, really good at being attuned during sex together, and both his body and mine had plenty of energy left to spend on each other. So instead of turning in even a little early, we made use of the full expanse of that king sized bed for hours.

THIRTY-SEVEN

COLE

It was nearing dinnertime by the time we got back to Rockport. After napping, we headed to a relatively quiet meal with my family. Larissa's and Margo's in-laws all lived near Corpus, and they'd be spending most of their time until Christmas morning with those families. Meanwhile, Brendan and Ignatius took advantage of the fact that locals usually left them alone to go out with just their wives—once Brendan won the coin flip to claim everyone's favorite seafood shack for his date with Jeannie.

We saw Sarita briefly, while she teased Ignatius into appreciating the chance to eat the superior gumbo at the second-best seafood place. But then it was just my parents, Emmeline, Andi, and me. For a Dunway dinner table, it was practically deserted.

Which was the kind of setting that made Emmers chatty. She filled us in on her job search, some drama with her friend group, "And," she said, turning to Andi, "I ran into Elliot leaving the grocery store this morning, and gave him a tin of our cookies, and thanked him for listening to our apology. So. Thanks for prompting all that."

They gave Emmeline's arm a quick squeeze. "Sounds like a positive encounter."

"I hope he thinks so. It'll take more than my delicious chocolate crinkle cookies and a few texts to prove our about-face is real, but it's worth any effort."

"You're talking about Cole's Elliot?" Dad asked, with a glance between me and Andi that suggested some confusion.

I did my best to explain without muttering anything like, "All of your children have been actively rude to the guy, who may be snide, but he has his reasons."

Mama's hand had taken mine during the telling. "And your Andi was the one who said something to put a halt to the things mis hijes have been saying? Things that made this state, this community, an even more hostile place for the LGBTQ plus community?"

I warmed at her gender-neutral calling out of her children; I'd overheard Emmers talking to the elders about inclusive Spanish over tamale making. And I sent thanks into the universe, again, to have these fierce, loving, accepting parents in my life. "They were. And we've all taken heed. It was an important message."

"Gracias, Andi. You get the last slice of cake if you want it."

They took it, as they deserved. Probably they also suspected if they didn't, Emmers and I would bicker over it. Because even as I immersed myself in a new, grown-ass relationship, being around my family for any length of time inevitably erased some of my maturity. Hence my failure to see past Elliot's attitude to the greater implications of our petty, alienating behavior.

The rest of the weekend stayed relaxed. Andi and I took a bird tour at Aransas Pass the next day, after I'd put on a crockpot of chili for Christmas Eve dinner. Later, Emmers, Andi, Ignatius, and I spent the evening tidying the house and staging packages around the Christmas tree while most everyone else went to church. Seeing Andi relaxed enough to banter with Ignatius about the aesthetics of grouping all the gift-bag presents to one side versus interspersing them with the wrapped ones, my heart tugged.

They clocked my sappy smile and asked, "What's up?"

I stopped resisting another stolen kiss, though I did tug them into a corner first so no one would complain that our making out was in their way. "I like how well you fit here. How well you fit in my life."

"Hmm, same. Here's what I like about it. I fit in, but not because I'm contorting myself to do so. You—all of you Dunways, but mostly it's just you—make me feel like you've created an Andi-shaped space for me. It feels a little precarious. I'm not going to lie. I'm not used to having that. Even my cat is supposedly as happy to have the cousin around as he was to be with me."

"I can't wait to meet Moscato."

"Ha. He'll probably love you most and then I'll be demoted further in his eyes."

I stroked their brow, smoothed back the strand of hair that had strayed from their topknot. "There's something Dad and Mama said to me, back when I was first telling them my name and gender. It was ... let me think how they put it. They said it wasn't water, or vapor, or ice that they loved. They loved H_2O, no matter the state it took. And that's the same way I feel about you. You can be a saltwater tide sometimes, or an icicle, or snowfall. Whatever you need to be, whatever your shape or your state, you fit with me, because you're H_2O."

I didn't say how much I love H_2O. It wasn't necessary

for the analogy to go around exposing my heart quite that much.

Maybe Andi could draw their own conclusions, but instead of pressing anything more into the open, they snuggled into me. And I was right: they and I, we fit.

THIRTY-EIGHT

ANDI

Even before we made it to the family house on Christmas morning, Estella and Cass video called from Ft. Worth. It wasn't a long call; Evelyn popped in after three minutes to tell me, "Merry Christmas," while making it clear my sisters should report to the car for the drive to church.

But they said they'd call again in two days, so I could give them a tour of my apartment and introduce Moscato. They signed off by blowing kisses to me, and to Cole.

He understood enough of my mood after that to take my hand and walk quietly beside me. We drew to a halt just out of sight of his house.

"You ready for this?"

I gave myself a moment. But then I grinned, and I meant it. "Did I tell you Scorch gave me ten bucks to back Alfie's French toast?"

"That's it? Ten bucks? He has a Grammy."

"I know, right? I can't decide whether to rat him out to Brendan, or stay quiet and work it into a CKC-K story."

Cole bounced in place. "The fic. It's got to be the fic."

"Okay, but if I tell Brendan today, I get to see all their reactions."

"Easy. Put it in next Christmas's interlude, and we can watch the fireworks up close and personal."

I'd been about to head inside, but froze at Cole's offhand certainty that I'd be in Rockport twelve months in the future.

At my reflexive acceptance that it was likely.

Whatever my face read, Cole took it as a chance to wrap me in one of his comforting hugs. "Too much?"

I kissed his cheek, which was flushed above his beard. From emotion, rather than cold, since it'd come on so fast. "Not too much. Kind of weirdly not too much. Is there any way to work it so we get the cottage two years in a row?"

He huffed. "A combination of wheedling, sneakiness, and bribery via months-long group text, maybe. We can try."

"I'll spend the day gathering blackmail. This baked French toast battle is as good a place to start as any." I half-feared, half-anticipated, having my own contributions to the Dunway dossier.

Maybe more on the glee side than the fear side. Knowing I could lob good-natured accusations at them all and no one would mind my vindictive side? Kind of a gleeful fact to tuck into my soul.

Larissa's family pulled in then, so we went to help them carry in children and food and whatever else couldn't be left in the SUV for a few hours. We entered to a predictably cheerful chaos, everyone hugging and catching up on whatever happened in the few nights spent apart. Alfie Junior was the center of attention during the Dunway tradition of everyone opening one gift before brunch, passing out the presents for a few minutes before getting distracted by the big box that was his first of the morning.

After breakfast—Alfie Senior won the bake-off, but Brendan's dish was the first to be gobbled up by the crowd —we settled in for the rest of the gift exchange. There was some kind of semi-annual debate, far as I could tell, about drawing names instead of everyone buying for everyone else, that seemed unlikely to be resolved. I kept being given gifts: insulated gloves, a touristy Rockport t-shirt, Christmas socks. Ignatius brought me a box and Sarita moved close to take pictures as I opened it.

"We had to go over to Luis's to borrow his model paints to customize it," Ignatius said, his face a tragedy mask. "So you better love it."

It was an ornament that had probably started out as a school bus, but they'd redone it to match Scorch's tour bus, complete with a not-bad rendition of his publicity photo. Instead of his stage name over the red flame background, it said *Perseus* on the side of the bus.

"Oh my god, y'all. This is amazing."

"Wait, you gave the bus to Andi already? Did they love it? I bet they loved it." Brendan slid Sarita out of the way and asked me, "How much do you love it?"

"A million light-years' worth of love."

He fist-bumped Ignatius. "Knew it."

"We're the best," Ignatius agreed. "I'm practically as amazing as Captain Kindle Cable-Kitching herself."

Everyone had me pass the ornament around, and I dipped my head to keep any tears out of sight of Sarita's camera.

"Well, that makes my present comparatively boring," Cole said, handing me an oblong box.

"Hang on, do mine at the same time."

I found the bag with the journals and pens I'd bought him. I couldn't focus on his reaction, though, between the lingering tenderness of the bus ornament and this … completely magical, completely me blazer he'd given me. It was a deep blue, with feathered white lapels and a stylized print of cranes flying across the back panel, and I wanted to wear it immediately.

"How on earth did you find this?" I stood and slipped it on. It was snug over my sweater, but would be perfect over a shirt.

Cole looked up from cradling his new journals, smug grin firmly in place. "Call it luck or call it fate. It was in the resale shop and I couldn't resist. Looks great on you."

"Take a picture so I can see." I handed over my phone.

"Bossy," he said, but mildly, so I could hope his family didn't pick up on any innuendo. "And thank you. These are perfect journals."

"For all your lists."

"Yes, I got that very subtle dig."

I tumbled into his lap, smiling towards all the Dunway cameras that aimed at us once the bus was back in my hands. And then smiling only for Cole, and for me, and for a holiday that shattered every one of my expectations and left me free to find myself.

And to find what felt entirely like love.

And to let myself be found in return.

EPILOGUE

COLE

I screeched to a halt outside the airport gift shop. "Do I need to get this for Spencer?"

Andi followed my pointing finger to the set of blocks featuring Philly landmarks. "You got him blocks for his birthday," they reminded me.

"Yes, but not these."

Andi turned to their sisters. "I warned you. Don't say I didn't warn you." Cass giggled and Estella rolled her eyes.

Evelyn had allowed Cass and Stell to fly up and stay with us for a few days between the end of their school term and the start of our own Christmas trip. We'd shown them the sights, adding street curling and eating raclette to the panoply of Ennis traditions. Now we were all flying back to Houston, where we'd drop off the girls before spending a few days in Rockport.

Not in the cottage this time, but we'd already battled Moscato to create a blanket fort in our apartment and watched *The Muppet Christmas Carol* with the girls.

Andi's backpack held their CKC-K story about the bake-off bribery, which they'd had printed and bound for my brothers-in-law. For the rest of our presents, we trusted the airline would send them through to Texas in our checked bags. With the kids actively judging me, I decided against going overboard or hedging my gift-giving bets. "Fine. Andi's warning was maybe timely, but I won't gripe about it, because I'm gracious like that."

Estella's 'I doubt everything you've ever said' thirteen-year-old face was all too familiar, after spending four nights with us. So was Andi's 'it's so convenient to have my sister here so I don't have to state the obvious' expression.

I linked arms with them both. "I hereby forego the blocks. What's our gate number?"

Cassiopeia not only had it memorized, but had used the time while I contemplated toys to figure out which direction to go when I tipped my chin at her to lead us.

Andi snugged up next to me. "Excited to be heading home?"

I turned to them as the girls spread out in search of seating at our gate. "I mean, to see everybody? Yeah, of course. But if you'll excuse me getting so full of holiday sentiment, hon ... as long as I'm with you, I'm home."

The way their face softened—it got me every time. It reminded me how fortunate we were to have figured out how to work our way into a life together. One that was full of laughter, and community, and trust in each other that as we moved through our days, we would always choose to approach challenges together.

They didn't need to say any of that. They didn't even need to say, "I love you," though they did. I stole a quick kiss, and they gave me back a longer one in return.

When we rejoined their sisters, I let the girls get away with grumbling about my constantly being so affectionate, so enthusiastic, about Andi Ennis, the stunning love of my life. Because all of us knew the truth: Andi and I were binary stars, and together, we glowed.

* * *

THANKS FOR JOURNEYING into a bright future with Away With a Stranger. *Reviews are an invaluable tool for authors, and I'd love to get your honest review at any of the following places, or others of your choosing:*

*Stores * Goodreads * Bookbub*

FOR A COMPLETE BOOK list and more, keep scrolling. You can also check out Sarita & Scorch's meet-ouch in the enclosed sample chapter.
   Happy reading!
   -Melanie

Acknowledgments

This is my fifteenth book, and I'm as giddy about it as I was with the first ones. It's so amazing to me that I get to write romance as my job, but even more amazing that I have so much support in my life that allows this to be true.

My writing communities are essential to my motivation, brainstorming, occasional griping, and constant inspiration. If you see me on Slack or Discord, know that I also see you, and thank you for being vital to me.

I was once again lucky to have David Pena as my sensitivity editor. While no one person represents a whole, of course, I've learned so much and been so encouraged by David's feedback and appreciation for my characters. His help gave depth and life to Cole and to Andi; any failures of representation are, of course, mine.

The most constant constant in my life is Robert; we reached our thirtieth anniversary this year, and are still inclined to adore each other. As all my time steeped in the romance genre proves, it's not just the fun falling for each other, but the ways that, having fallen, we choose to keep making it work that matters. Big stuff, little stuff, amazing kids, ten thousand cups of tea; it's all gone into building a gorgeous life together.

About the Author

Melanie Greene lives in a tiny woodland cottage in a big skyscraper city, with her husband and kids and pets and plants and all the people inhabiting her imagination.

For more info, visit her at www.melaniegreene.com, where you can sign up for her newsletter to access new releases and bonus content.

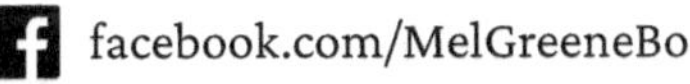 facebook.com/MelGreeneBooks

instagram.com/melaniegreeneauthor